WHEN SHADOWS CALL

A SHADOW CELL THRILLER

ERNEST DEMPSEY

ENCLAVE PUBLISHING

1

LOCATION: CLASSIFIED

Adriana's eyes peeled open, the lids grating her eyeballs like sandpaper. The darkness didn't dispel. She blinked more rapidly to rid her mind of the fog and—she hoped—the inability to see, but it was no use.

It took another few seconds for her to feel the bag wrapped around her head and neck. In the pervasive haze filling her vision and thoughts, she hadn't noticed it at first.

The next thing she realized was the restricting pain in her wrists and ankles.

Tied to a chair, she thought. *With a bag over my head. Wonder who I pissed off this time.*

She had no recollection of what happened or who could have done this, but one thought kept resonating in her mind: she'd kill whoever was responsible.

Her muscles strained against her bonds, over and over, until she realized it was an exercise in futility. Whoever had tied the knots wasn't fooling around. They intended to keep her exactly where she was.

That brought up another question: *Where am I?*

For the time being, there was no way to know.

A door creaked from somewhere across the void, and she sat up a little straighter.

"I see you're awake," a man's voice said. His accent was distinctly English, refined, probably raised by a prominent family that had a permanently scheduled tea time every day of their lives.

She didn't answer. Her only response was a fierce scowl the man could not yet see.

"I'm certain you have a thousand questions running through that pretty head of yours. Why are you here? Who brought you? Where is here?"

"I suppose you're going to give me some answers?" she spat through clenched teeth.

The black sack on her head was suddenly yanked away, and she looked up to find herself in a tiny square-shaped room, surrounded by cinder blocks and a gray ceiling and floor. A single fluorescent light gave off the only illumination in the space and reinforced the overwhelming feeling of sterility—and isolation.

"Of course I am, Miss Villa. Would you mind if I called you Adriana?"

The man speaking to her was tall, probably a few inches over six feet. His frame was lanky but imposing—possibly due to the thousand-dollar suit covering his body. His hairline had receded to just beyond the tip of his forehead and appeared to have halted, leaving a distinctive look and shape to his head. His nose was long and pointy, matching the snide grin on his lips.

"I don't care what you call me. The second you let me go will be the next-to-last second of your life."

The man's grin widened slightly. "I knew you were the right woman for the job, Adriana," he said as he pulled up a metal chair from a few feet away and eased into the seat. "I have to say, I've heard so many good things about you. I've become quite a fan over the years."

"What are you talking about?" She strained against the ropes once more, vainly hoping it would be the time their strength gave way. It wasn't.

He crossed one leg over the other and folded his hands on his thigh. "The rogue thief who steals lost masterpieces and restores them to their proper owners. I have to say, it must be very invigorating, albeit dangerous."

"What do you want? Why am I here?"

"I've heard you're typically direct, to the point, Miss Villa...sorry, did you say it was all right for me to call you Adriana?"

She sneered but didn't offer a reply.

"I'll take that as a yes. No need for formality. After all, if you decide to play by our rules, you'll have a different title."

The comment caused her eyebrows to pinch together in confusion.

"My name, Adriana, isn't important. For now, you may call me the Director."

"Director? I already have a friend who's a director."

"Yes, I am aware of your friendship with Director Starks at the Axis agency. Tidy little operation they run over there. I also admire their work, though they occasionally cross paths with us, which I don't need to tell you has a tendency to complicate things."

He said over there. Based on the accent and his reference about the location of Axis headquarters, that meant she was probably still in Europe.

Memories flooded her mind. She'd been in Munich searching for clues to a lost painting. Something had happened. A man. She remembered seeing a guy in a dark trench coat fifty feet down the sidewalk. The sight had stood out because the temperature was unusually hot for that time of year. Most of the locals were in shorts and tank tops or T-shirts. Even the businesspeople carried their jackets in their arms to ease the sweltering heat.

The man in the trench coat approached her. He'd had a menacing look on his face underneath darkly tinted sunglasses. She'd been so focused on the perceived threat that she didn't see someone else come up from behind her. The last thing she remembered was a sudden prick on the side of her left arm.

"Since you prefer to not beat around the bush, Adriana, I will extend the same courtesy to you so as to save time for the both of us."

"That would be lovely. Then I can get back to my plan to kill you."

For a second, he seemed amused. "I assure you, Adriana, we are on the same team. I'm hoping we can make that an official standing."

There it was again, a reference to some kind of offer. *What was he getting at?*

"I have to admit," he said. "You are something of a difficult woman to track down, even for me. Luckily, we have a common ally."

"Common ally?"

"Yes," he said, raising his eyebrows. "You come highly recommended, by the way."

"By who?"

He raised his leg and crossed it over the other to ease the circulation. "Let me be blunt, Adriana. We are part of a top-secret agency known as Shadow Cell. We know about your background: born just outside of Madrid, fluent in several languages and even a few dialects, assets all over the globe including property, bonds, money, and even bullion."

She ignored the last part and focused on the word he kept using as if it made everything clear. "We?"

"Yes," he elongated the word for dramatic effect. "We are a small operation, much like the one your friend Director Starks runs in Atlanta."

"So, you're spies, assassins, what?" she snarled.

He refolded his hands across his lap. "Both—when necessity requires. However, we do our best not to get involved in the intelligence-counterintelligence game. MI5, MI6, the CIA, NSA, they all have that covered and, for the most part, do a good job."

"That's debatable."

He allowed a quiet snort to escape his nose. "Indeed."

"If all those other agencies have everything covered, what is it you do, exactly?"

He drew a long breath. "Adriana, most of the world's agencies are constantly focused on each other. Sure, they monitor terrorist threats as best they can, but there is only so much they can do. Terrorist cells operate quite differently than governments."

"I'm aware of that. Get to the point."

The Director didn't flinch at her brusqueness. "We have received information that there is a new group of terrorists on the rise. They have a hierarchy of leaders across the globe who are—as we speak—setting up a network that will shake the very foundation of civilization."

"So? Take them out."

"Why do you think I'm talking to you?"

Her frown deepened. "No. I mean have one of your agents take them out."

"I wish it was that simple, Adriana. You see, Shadow Cell is relatively new. You will be our second field operative—should you decide to come work for us."

She pressed her back against the chair. "What?"

"Terrorist attacks have been on the rise since 2001, Miss Villa." He had returned, inexplicably, to formal address. "We never know where they're going to hit or when. Paris, Belgium, Germany, Barcelona, Finland—all were random places, and no one had a clue they were coming."

"That's what makes it terrorism," Adriana said, pointing out the obvious.

"Indeed."

"I still don't see what any of this has to do with me."

"We want you to infiltrate their network, take out the men in charge, and retrieve anything you can about how they operate. Your first mission is this man...." He clicked something in his palm, and an image appeared on the concrete wall to her left. It was a man with a thick black beard and dark, vapid eyes. The picture was taken of him next to a pool as he stared at a cell phone.

"Who is that?"

"Camir Asad," the Director said. "Their organization is called the Red Ring. I personally don't understand the name, though we have information that suggests it has something to do with an ancient prophecy."

She lifted an eyebrow.

"At any rate, Asad is one of the men in charge."

"Is he the leader?"

"No. He's one of the leaders, but the head of their network is unknown. We're hoping you can get him to give you more information about the rest of the men running the operation."

"So, you don't know anything?" Adriana didn't care if she came off as rude. She was tied to a friggin' chair.

"In a manner of speaking, I suppose," the Director said. "We know there are several of them because we captured one of their operatives in London early last month. He'd strolled into a train station with six pounds of explosives strapped to his chest. Apparently, his knowledge of electrical circuitry was less than stellar. The bomb didn't work, and he was apprehended without anyone being harmed. After some persuasion, he gave us Asad's name and laid out how their hierarchy works."

"It sounds like you have a handle on this. I hope it all works out well for you."

The Director bit his lower lip. "Adriana, you are—perhaps—the best thief in the world. You are able to get in and out of places without being detected, taking priceless relics from some of the most secure locations on the planet."

He was right about that. She'd broken into homes with million-dollar security systems, she'd cracked vaults, and she'd picked impossible locks—all for what she deemed a worthy cause.

"You're not asking me to steal things from people who stole them from others. You're asking me to kill."

"I'm asking you to do both, Adriana. Some of these men may have information, information we need to keep out of the hands of more powerful villains. Besides, it's not like you haven't killed before."

"I've never murdered anyone if that's what you're saying."

"If you don't take these men out, we'll have to find someone else to do it. No one is as adept as you at getting in and out of places without being noticed. By eliminating these men, you'll be saving countless other lives all over the world."

It was a classic argument. Kill one to save twenty. She still didn't like the idea.

"I'm sorry, Director. I have my own problems."

His lungs filled with air, and he exhaled slowly. "Yes, I'm aware of your issues with the syndicate."

This guy was full of surprises. *How in the world did he know about that?*

"You know about the syndicate?" There was no effort to mask her astonishment.

"We are aware of their actions. While they're something of a secret society, their members are often in the public eye. They're easy enough to find. If you help us," he said, "we will help you."

The deal sounded good, but Adriana wasn't one to accept help from people, especially strangers who drugged her and took her to an undisclosed location only to tie her to a chair. "So, you want me to take out these terrorists, and then you will help me eliminate the syndicate?"

"That's the deal, Adriana. Of course, you will receive hazard pay for your time." He paused and could tell she was about to protest, so he cut her off. "I know you don't need the money. I'm quite aware of your family's fortune. Still, it wouldn't be right to not pay you."

She couldn't argue with that.

"What makes you think I need your help?"

"The syndicate is a massive organization with unlimited funding. At this very moment, they have assets in play, searching for you."

That part she assumed, but hearing it was unsettling.

"When they find you—and they will find you—they will eliminate you like a weed in a garden. There is nowhere you can hide from them forever."

"I'll have to think about it," she said after a moment of thought. "I have a few things I need to take care of first."

"Very well," he said as he stood and turned to leave. "My assistant will show you out." He placed a white business card in the chair's seat

and walked toward the door. "I do hope you'll say yes. Terribly difficult to find a person with your particular skill set in this day and age."

"You said someone referred me to you," Adriana said. "Who?"

The Director stopped and pivoted around. A wry grin crossed his
face. "You know her," he said. "Your friend June is one of us."

He disappeared through the door, leaving her alone with the
shocking revelation and a million thoughts running through
her head.

2

LIVERPOOL, ENGLAND

Adriana stepped through the creaky metal door and out into a drizzling rain. She pulled her thin jacket tight around her arms. It did little to keep the cool air from her skin.

She was next to the River Mersey, that much she knew. From the looks of things, the docks hadn't been used in a long time. The warehouses appeared to have been abandoned long ago. A few rusted forklifts and flat carts sat silently along one of the crumbling brick walls.

It was a dreary setting and a perfect location for a secret group of assassins—or whatever they were. No one would think that underneath the cracking streets and derelict buildings a group of people was running some sort of counterterrorism unit.

"I'm sorry I didn't tell you sooner," a familiar voice said from around the corner.

Adriana didn't turn her head. She knew someone was there. In fact, she'd assumed it was June. Her instincts, it seemed, were as sharp as ever.

June stepped around the corner of the building. She was wearing a black trench coat and held a clear umbrella over her head.

"I knew there was more to you than met the eye," Adriana said. "Your precision, your movements...something about you screamed confidence underneath that fearful disguise."

June shrugged. "The fear isn't a disguise. It's real. If you aren't at least a little afraid in my line of work, then you'll get sloppy. Fear keeps us alive. It keeps us sharp."

She stepped close and offered to share the umbrella with her friend.

"I assume Tommy doesn't know about all this," Adriana said.

"No. And it needs to stay that way."

"Tommy's a smart guy, June. He'll figure it out eventually."

Tommy Schultz was June's boyfriend. Head of the International Archaeological Agency in Atlanta, he was often abroad, scouring the globe for lost artifacts or recovering relics for a government. Occasionally, he did work for private entities, though he preferred to steer clear of those for personal reasons.

Adriana had met Tommy and his best friend, Sean Wyatt, while investigating a lead in Las Vegas. She'd saved their lives, helped them with the case, and in the end started dating Sean.

"I'm sure he'll figure something out sooner or later," June said.

"That's good. Every solid relationship should be founded in some form of dishonesty. Is it even a real relationship? Do you have feelings for him?"

"Of course I do, Adriana. Everything I have with Tommy is very real. I love him. Which is why I can't tell him about this. Not yet. He'll freak out."

"You're right about that."

"Exactly. So, between you and me, I need to keep this under wraps for a while. Just until I can figure out what to tell him."

"And how to tell him."

"Right."

Adriana stared out at the Mersey and shook her head. "So what, the researcher thing is a ruse? A side gig? What?"

"It's part of what I do for the agency. While Sean and Tommy do what they do to preserve history, I do what I do to help keep dangerous parts of history out of the wrong hands."

"Dangerous parts of history?"

"Think about the events of the last several years, Adriana. Our boyfriends have gotten into no end of trouble. Often, that trouble has global implications. Known terrorists—even the ones Tommy and Sean haven't encountered—are constantly looking for something that will give them more power. And it's not just terrorists. Think about every villain Tommy and Sean have encountered since Tommy started the IAA. Lot of people bent on bad intentions."

"So, you're trying to stay one step ahead of those types?"

June nodded. "That's one of my main roles, yes. It was no accident that I met your friends. The research gig in Germany was just a cover. I was there on assignment."

Adriana stood there silently, still looking out over the murky water.

"Look," June said after waiting, "I know this is sudden. And I'm sorry for being dishonest before. The truth is we need you. I've seen what you can do in the field. You have a skill set that very few possess."

"I have my own thing."

"I know. And it's an admirable hobby...or whatever you call it. But the art can wait, Adriana. The world can't. It needs heroes, guardians to watch over the innocent from the shadows. It's time for you to use your abilities to help keep them safe. If you don't do it, who will?"

Adriana didn't respond immediately. She thought for another moment and then sighed. "You been practicing that?"

"Little bit." June grinned.

"I'm no hero."

"Which is the first prerequisite to being one."

"So what, we travel the world hunting down terrorists and bad guys? Doesn't leave a lot of time for our guys."

"You've made do in the past, as have I. They're out of the country most of the time anyway. Honestly, I doubt they'll notice."

"If we end up dead or held hostage somewhere, I'm pretty sure they'd notice."

"Then we better stay sharp."

"What happens if I say yes?" Adriana asked. "Is there a training program or something? Because I have to be honest: I don't do that sort of stuff."

"No. You don't have to do anything like that. If you say yes, we begin immediately."

"And if I say no?"

June averted her gaze and matched Adriana's, staring out at the rapidly flowing river. "Then nothing. You go back to your hobby and dating Sean and whatever else you do in life. No harm. You'll never hear from us again."

"Just like that, huh?"

"Yep. Just like that."

"No hunting me down to kill me because I know about your operation?"

"We're not in the business of killing good people, Adriana."

"Just the bad ones."

"Let me know if you're interested," June said as she turned to walk away. "Your talents would be a huge asset for us. I know that your work with the lost art is important to you, but think of the lives you could save. This is an incredible opportunity."

June strolled away and disappeared around the corner, leaving Adriana alone in the rain once more.

"Did she just walk away?" Adriana muttered. Then she shook her head, realizing she still had no clue as to where she was.

She turned and started trotting down the asphalt toward the corner where her friend had gone. Adriana rounded the corner and was surprised to find June standing by a black Jaguar sedan.

"That was fast," June said with a smile.

"I wasn't saying yes just yet," Adriana corrected. "I just have no idea where I am."

"Liverpool, England."

"I figured that much."

"Get in, and I'll take you wherever you want to go. No pressure. I've given you my best sales pitch."

"I was in Munich," Adriana said. "You gonna drive me there?"

"I'll get you to the nearest train station."

Close enough.

Adriana slid into the passenger side as June climbed into the driver's seat.

"Sorry for getting your car wet," Adriana said.

"Not a problem. It's a company car."

June shifted the vehicle into gear and sped away, kicking loose bits of rock and debris out from the rear tires.

She guided the car through the docks and back to a chain-link fence that started opening automatically just before they reached it.

"How is it funded?" Adriana blurted out.

June steered the car to the right and accelerated. New raindrops splattered on the windshield as soon as the wipers slung the old ones away.

"We're primarily funded by the crown," June explained. "The royals don't need all the money they're allotted. They haven't ever needed that much. Most of the things they would have to pay for are taken care of by the government. So, we diverted some of their funding into our coffers."

"You stole the queen's money?" Adriana looked impressed.

"No," June said with a laugh. "She's the one who approved the allotment."

"Oh."

"The queen understands that times have changed since she was younger. Enemies of the crown and of humanity in general are no longer marching across a battlefield, carrying a flag that identifies their loyalty. They hide in the shadows, in basements, crumbling buildings, or sometimes in plain sight. You never know where they're going to hit next. It's our job to find out that information and shut them down before they can hurt anyone."

June was right. Times had changed significantly since the queen ascended the throne. Every major war in history had pitted two sides against one another, each clearly distinguished. It wasn't that way anymore.

"That's why we're called Shadow Cell," June said. "We must get in where the enemy lives, operate in their backyard, take the fight to them. Not only that; we must make acts of terrorism unthinkable."

Adriana's forehead wrinkled. "Unthinkable?"

"We are messengers, Adriana. We send a message to anyone who would consider attacking innocents. If they bomb a church, we burn a terrorist training camp. They run a truck through a crowd of people? We hang their leaders in plain sight. We set an example. It isn't always pretty. But it is the world we live in. It's time for those with evil intentions to face equal punishment."

"Sounds a bit vigilante if you ask me."

June shrugged. "The law fails every single day. The United Nations is useless. And the governments of the world are tied up in boardrooms, bickering about their own issues, all of them looking out for their individual concerns."

Adriana gazed out the window. She remembered talking to Sean so many times about his experience with the Axis agency. He swore he'd never go back to it—that the danger, intrigue, and living a life on the run weren't worth it.

Then again, it seemed he'd gone from the flames into the fire by moving to IAA. He and Tommy found themselves in no end of trouble.

"Sean used to talk to me about his time with Axis," Adriana said in an absent tone. "He claimed that it was never-ending, that when one mission was completed, another one was there waiting. Your director said that he only wants my help to take down the Red Ring. We both know he wants more than that. He wants me to be a full-time agent. I have a personal life now, people I care about. I saw what this sort of work did to my father, how it changed him. He couldn't be there when my mother needed him—when she was dying. I don't want to be involved with something that will take me away from the people and things I care about. Life is too short."

June listened quietly as she drove the car. She turned into a train station on the right and parked as close to the entrance as possible.

She shifted the vehicle into park and looked over at her passenger. "I understand, Adriana. Truly, I do. Someday, perhaps there won't be a need for our kind anymore. I will be very happy to see that day come. Until then, however, the ones who defend humanity against the forces of evil—ones who can—must choose to take a stand or watch from the sidelines knowing they could do something to stop the mayhem but didn't. I choose to stand. I don't judge you either way. And we will still be friends. I just thought I would offer."

Adriana gave a feeble nod. "I understand. Thank you for the invitation. Although you guys might want to rethink the whole kidnapping recruits and putting bags over their heads. I have a phone, you know."

"Yeah, I agree. It isn't a very cordial way of bringing someone in for a job interview."

Adriana opened the door and put a foot out onto the wet pavement. "Thanks again, June. But I think I'll pass. I have a lot going on right now, especially with Sean. I have a chance to make something with him that I've never had with another man. I don't want to blow it."

"I totally understand. I don't want to mess things up with Tommy either. Do me a favor? Please don't tell him. I know that eventually I'll have to come clean, but not yet. After all, it is a secret agency."

"My lips are sealed," Adriana said. "Good luck, June. Be careful out there."

"You too."

Adriana closed the door and watched her friend pull away. She stared at the sedan until it disappeared around the corner of the train station before turning and walking up to the ticket office.

After purchasing her pass, she entered the station and found a bench on the platform where a small group of people gathered to wait on their train. She pulled her phone out of her pocket and sat down. Her notes from the case she'd been working on were still there. Thankfully, the people in charge of Shadow Cell hadn't permanently confiscated her belongings or altered them—not that she knew of, at least.

"Now, where was I?" she muttered to herself as she scanned a picture of a painting that had disappeared at the beginning of World War II. "Where might you be?"

3

PARIS, FRANCE

Adriana sat at a cafe along the street in the 10th Arrondissement. Bicyclists pedaled by in a casual rhythm, clearly in no hurry to get wherever they were going. Pedestrians strolled by at a similar pace, leisurely and carefree. The high late morning sun beamed down brightly, and despite a chill in the fall air Adriana didn't feel the cold in her black hoodie.

She traced her right index finger along the lines of an article on her computer. It was a newspaper piece, written more than forty years prior about a piece art that went missing from a private collection. The collector—an Italian national—had failed to give the exact details about the painting, though he claimed it was a priceless masterpiece.

It was a strange story, to say the least. Why not tell the insurance companies, the banks, and the authorities the name of the painting's creator? And what of the title? It seemed like a foolish thing to not give enough details to aid in the recovery of the painting.

Foolish—unless the Italian collector was doing his best to hide the fact that he'd somehow procured a piece of art that belonged to someone else.

The man's name was Marco Conte according to the article. He'd built up a vast fortune immediately following World War II, taking advantage of huge gaps in the market left after Mussolini's fascist regime had been overthrown.

His main source of revenue had been textiles, but after a little digging Adriana learned that the guy had a darker side.

He dealt in the arms trade, shipping weapons to rebels in various countries during a time when everyone felt like they could win their freedom and, if not freedom, something far more important: power.

Conte didn't care where the weapons went. And according to her research, he didn't seem to mind that many of the guns and ammunition he sold had a high rate of malfunction.

She figured it was karma that he was killed on a private shooting range when the gun he was using misfired and put a batch of shrapnel through his face and brain.

It took hours, days even, searching through the scores of electronically stored microfilm and old records before she found the image she was looking for. When she did find it, she knew that Conte was the man she'd been searching for.

That still didn't explain where the painting was now, nearly forty years after it had been taken from him. Adriana had a source here in Paris that could help, someone who'd worked as an assistant curator at the Louvre. The woman also had plenty of connections in the criminal underbelly of Paris. If anyone had information concerning the missing Conte painting, it would be her.

Adriana picked up the phone from the table and started looking through the contacts. She passed June's name and paused for a second. It had been two days since the bizarre encounter with her friend. Two days since being abducted and waking up in an abandoned warehouse somewhere in Liverpool. It seemed forever ago, like a distant faux memory from a dream.

How June had managed to keep her exploits a secret from Tommy, Adriana didn't know, but sooner or later a secret that big would come out.

She kept scrolling through the names and found the one she was looking for. She started to tap it when she heard a low boom. It was in the distance, probably a half mile away. Then the earth shook. The table vibrated, and her coffee cup jiggled on its saucer.

Adriana and the other patrons looked up, befuddled. A second later, everyone started looking around at each other, checking faces to see if anyone had an explanation.

The first clue as to what happened was a pillar of black smoke that appeared over the buildings across the street. Then there was another low boom, this time a little closer than the first.

Adriana sprang from her seat and turned to face the cafe's manager who'd come out onto the patio and was staring at the strange site along with everyone else.

"Do you have a basement?" she asked in hurried French.

"Yes," he answered in kind. "Why?"

"Get all these people down there. Now!"

"Why?"

"It's an attack!"

Some of the patrons rushed into the building with the manager. Others sprinted for their cars, thinking a quick getaway was the best option. Some sat in their chairs, faces washed pale with shock, unable to move. There were at least a dozen like that.

No way she could help all of them. She turned and sprinted across the suddenly gridlocked street, heading for the sounds of chaos.

She jumped and slid over the hood of a car, landed on her feet on the other side in mid-stride, and kept going. The driver yelled something in French. She was too far away to hear him clearly, but she assumed he'd hurled some kind of profanity.

The clouds of dark smoke billowed into the sky. Screams filled the air and echoed through the canyons of concrete, steel, and glass. The arrondissement had gone from a peaceful sector of the city to Armageddon. Most of the people she encountered were running the opposite direction. Adriana didn't blame them. She, on the other hand, wasn't wired that way. She had to help however she could.

It was another full three blocks before she found the first signs of what happened. As she rounded the last corner at the border where the 10th and 11th Arrondissements met, she saw the remains of a compact car amid a raging fire. Sirens filled the air, but as yet only one cop had arrived on the scene and appeared to be helpless in the midst of the disaster.

Bodies were strewn everywhere. A quick sweep of the area told Adriana there were at least twenty casualties, and that was only on this side of the car. There was no way of knowing what had happened on the other side.

She instantly assessed the situation.

The car was parked next to the sidewalk, mere feet from a sidewalk cafe not unlike the one she'd just left. *Not a car accident.* Based on the blast, the charred building next to the wreckage, and the number of casualties, there was no questioning what happened.

This was a terrorist attack.

An ambulance roared around the corner and skidded to a stop. The paramedics rushed to the closest victims and began checking their vitals. Adriana knew the ones they left on the ground were already dead. Their job was to help the living. The dead were beyond saving.

She saw the smoke from the second explosion. It was a few blocks away. She imagined the scene there was much like this one.

Her heart sank, and she swallowed hard. Two more police cars arrived along with three fire engines. People were yelling orders now, collecting those who were standing nearby. Most of them had tears in their eyes, streaming down their cheeks. Some were in shock, unable to grasp what had just happened.

Amid the anarchy, Adriana saw something strange out of the corner of her eye. She twitched, turning her head toward the movement. It was something in a building across the street on the corner. A curtain moved. It was subtle, hardly noticeable, but she'd seen it. The window was open, and she could see a set of fingers holding it back as if waiting for something.

The threat wasn't over yet.

While emergency crews flooded the crowded street, Adriana charged toward the entrance of the building where she'd seen the movement in the window. It was four stories up. There was no way she could get there in time.

She saw a gendarme running toward the scene and grabbed him by the arm. "There's a sniper," she said. "Get this area clear."

He looked at her with puzzled eyes and then shook her hand free. She'd spoken in perfect French, so she knew he understood. Apparently, he wasn't going to take advice from a civilian—much less a tourist.

Adriana ran to the entrance and hurried through the door. Her head turned rapidly one direction and then the other until she found the elevators. That wouldn't be good. If there was a shooter up there, he could have booby-trapped or disabled them.

She didn't have a second to lose.

"Stairs it is."

By the time she reached the fourth floor, the top of her legs burned and her calves were tight, but she didn't slow down. She barged through the door and into the fourth-floor hallway. It took a second of looking down both ends of the hall before she got her bearings. She ran to the right, heading for what she believed was the apartment where the shooter was hiding.

At the end of the hall the corridor came to a T. She turned right again and moved as fast as possible on the tips of her toes. The floor creaked as she passed the next-to-last door, and she froze for a second. She grimaced, hoping the noise wasn't audible inside the apartments.

Not that it mattered. If they didn't hear that, they were going to hear it when she kicked down the door.

Adriana pulled out her compact 9mm Springfield she'd kept tucked away under her hoodie. The French wouldn't approve of the firearm, much less the small arsenal she had back at her hotel. They were sticklers about that sort of thing. Most European cops were.

She knew bad people were armed. Adriana figured it was imperative that the playing field be leveled.

She made it to the last door and held her weapon to the side as she took a step back and sized up how much force it would need.

Some people made the mistake of driving their shoulder into doors to knock them down. Doing so had caused more than a few shoulder separations, dislocations, and even a broken clavicle or two. She'd heard the stories and had no intentions of being so careless.

They were probably the standard deadbolt-and-doorknob lock, which gave two points of resistance. The three hinges on the left were older and thin, probably just as likely to give way as the locks on the other side.

Either way, Adriana had to make sure the door caved on the first blow.

She reared back, took a big step forward, and drove the heel of her boot into the center of the door.

It shuddered and then blew open with a heavy thud, swung around hard, and slammed into the wall on the other side. Adriana burst through and into the apartment. She didn't bother taking in the bare white walls, the sparse furniture, the kitchen, or what kind of faux wood flooring was under her feet. The only thing she cared about was the guy in the corner window, holding a rifle with a scope on the top and a suppressor on the barrel's end.

She aimed her weapon, but her entrance had startled the shooter. He jumped away from the window and rolled behind a small wooden table as Adriana fired.

The bullet thumped into the wall just beyond his left foot. A second later, he returned the favor, firing two shots just over her head as Adriana dove to her left behind the kitchen counter.

She'd only caught his face for a second, but it was easy to tell the gunman was of Middle Eastern descent. It was all too clear now. This was a massively coordinated terrorist attack. One bomber takes out civilians. Then a sniper picks off anyone coming to help.

Both were suicide jobs. Once the authorities realized what was going on, they'd track the sniper down and kill him. Arrest wasn't something this guy would allow. It was a one-way ticket.

His rifle popped again, shattering the corner of the counter near her left shoulder into a dozen pieces.

She slid to the right, stood up, and squeezed the trigger. Her first shot didn't have to be on target. It just had to be close enough to scare the guy. It did the job, and he ducked back behind his table. The next three shots plunked into the makeshift shield's surface.

The guy rolled around to the other side and whipped the long barrel around, letting loose another two rounds that narrowly missed their target.

Adriana ducked down again, counting in her head how many shots she'd fired and how many the sniper had used.

Based on her quick observation of his weapon's magazine, he still had several rounds left. She did as well. The problem wasn't ammunition. It was the power. His gun could blow through weak points in the counter's wall with devastating effect. He didn't have to be accurate. He just had to be lucky.

Another blast came from the other side of the apartment, and a bullet smashed through the counter door a foot from her shoulder.

She made a quick decision, got down on her belly, and crawled back to the corner of the kitchen counter. She slid across the floor and waited for a second. Another deafening shot thundered through the confined space. A huge chunk of the cabinet exploded, sending wooden splinters all over the floor.

Adriana rolled out from her place of refuge and unloaded six rounds at the overturned table. The gunman ducked for cover again, but this time Adriana pressed the issue, striding toward him with every trigger pull until she was nearly on top of him.

He sensed what was happening, slid out from behind his hiding spot, and whipped the barrel of his weapon around for the kill shot. In an instant, he knew there was no way he could get the aim right before she fired first, so he changed plans and kicked the corner of the table.

The furniture swung around, catching Adriana off guard. She jumped to the side and fired again at the same time the gunman did. Their rounds missed wildly, but now they were both in the open. They both squeezed their triggers simultaneously. The weapons clicked.

Adriana's eyes blazed as she glared at the killer. His eyes had a different look. It was distant, lifeless, set on one purpose.

She was first to her feet and rushed toward him. He rolled up to a standing position and braced himself as she launched through the air and planted her sole into his chest.

The blow knocked him back against the wall in a jarring thud, but he quickly recovered and blocked her right hook, then countered with a jab to her chin. Her head snapped to the side, and she reset quickly, just in time to take a hook to the jaw.

Adriana stumbled backward a few steps, partly from the dizzying shots she'd just taken and partly to regroup. She shook off the dazed feeling and raised her fists, twisting her body sideways to narrow the target area.

The killer sneered and reached behind his back. His hand returned to view with a large knife like those she'd seen military men carry. What she'd give for her tomahawk. He lunged forward, slashing the knife through the air to the right, left, and back to the right again. His balance was solid but not the best she'd seen. She jumped back, arching her spine to avoid the sharp metal tip. After avoiding the blade three times, she ran out of space and found herself backed up against the kitchen counter.

The guy sneered and stabbed the knife at her neck, but she ducked out of the way, grabbed his arm, and pulled with all her strength. The guy was strong, but with all her weight tugging down on the appendage he couldn't keep it up, no matter how hard he struggled. She felt his muscles tense as he tried to free the arm, which was just what she wanted.

Her fingers let go of the forearm and suddenly, the man's hand shot up toward him. He couldn't react fast enough against his own strain. The hand plunged the knife tip deep into his left shoulder.

He didn't scream or howl. The only sign of pain he let escape was a slight grunt through his lips. Then he looked down at the wound, yanked out the knife, and turned his attention back to Adriana.

She scrambled, retreating toward the open window, where the

curtains flapped in a gentle breeze. The myriad sounds coming from the street poured into the apartment.

The sniper charged toward her again, this time swinging the knife more wildly than before. He sneered with anger as he slashed one way and then the other. Adriana deftly dodged to the side, cupped her hands and slammed them into the guy's back. Then she leaned sideways and kicked hard. Her heel plowed into his kidneys, and the strength of the blow drove him toward the window. He stumbled forward, hands and arms flailing to regain balance. His forehead struck the glass pane and shattered it into a thousand pieces, a shower of broken shards raining onto to the sidewalk and street below.

He pulled his head back through the broken window, face and head streaked with oozing crimson. He wobbled, stunned. The knife hung loose in his hand. Adriana pounced. She grabbed him by the shirt and jerked him toward her, slamming her fist into his face over and over. By the third punch, the knife slipped from his fingers and clanked on the floor.

She didn't care. She hammered him again and again until his body grew heavy in her fist.

Then she pushed him to the window, letting his torso go through until he was only in the apartment from the waist down.

The guy's nose was a destroyed, bloody mess. His eyes were already swelling shut. He was barely conscious.

"Who planned this?" she shouted.

He didn't answer.

She pushed him a little farther out the window.

"I'll ask you one last time. Who planned this attack? Who's your leader?"

He gasped for breath as her grip tightened around the base of his neck. "The will of Allah."

He kicked his legs hard, driving his heels into her torso. The blow caught her off guard and sent her flopping onto the floor. The move freed him, but in the wrong direction. Maybe that's what he wanted.

The terrorist's feet slid over the windowsill and vanished from sight.

Adriana clambered to her feet and rushed back to the opening. The man was lying on the sidewalk, head smashed against the concrete and neck bent at a sickening angle. She swallowed hard and tried to catch her breath.

Gendarmes were rushing to the dead man on the sidewalk while dozens of other emergency crews continued their work, helping those who were still alive.

The war Adriana didn't want any part of had just come to her.

4
LONDON, ENGLAND

Adriana sat in a stiff black leather chair. The seat was out of place in the old foundry basement. A guard in a black suit and tie with a white shirt stood at the doorway with hands folded in front of his waist.

"You always wear sunglasses indoors?" she asked, trying to make polite conversation.

The guard didn't answer. He didn't even flinch.

"Not much for chitchat, huh?"

Again, he said nothing.

She decided not to bother the guy anymore. Instead, she folded her hands in her lap and returned to the events of the past forty-eight hours.

After killing the shooter in the apartment, Adriana had decided bypassing the authorities would be the best course of action. Since so many of the cops were busy taking care of the wounded and dead, getting around them wasn't too difficult. All she had to do was walk around looking stunned by the tragedy. Once she was out of the area, she picked up her pace and returned to the cafe where she'd been working.

The missing painting didn't seem so important anymore. In fact, it felt downright trivial. She'd retired to her hotel that evening amid all sorts of chaos. Most of the people in the building were doing everything they could to get out of town. The hotel manager was desperately trying to convince patrons not to leave, even offering them discounts on their rooms. Most of the tourists weren't having it. Only the businesspeople whose jobs depended on their being there remained.

Adriana didn't leave because she figured why bother.

The terrorist attacks were over for now, and the police presence throughout the city had been elevated considerably. From what she knew about these kinds of things, they happened in bursts not waves. There likely wouldn't be another attack in this city for a while.

Sadly, it was the third time in five years that terrorists had targeted Paris. Adriana considered the European attacks of recent years: Brussels, Barcelona, Manchester. No one had seen them coming.

Innocent lives were lost, and there wasn't anything anyone could do about it. Or was there?

As she sat alone in her dark hotel room, Adriana stared out at the beautiful old city. Blue lights flashed in the distance. Most of the sirens had ceased their screams. The mayor had declared a citywide curfew while investigators conducted a manhunt for other suspects they believed had something to do with the attacks.

She'd avoided the news, though catching updates on social media had kept her apprised of the goings-on. Her accounts were under false names and images to keep her as anonymous as possible, but she found the platforms were a good way to do some investigative work she couldn't perform otherwise.

It hadn't taken her long to make up her mind. In fact, before she even walked into the hotel to return to her room she'd already decided to phone the man who called himself the Director.

Before she did that, she took the liberty of sending June a text message. It was a simple two-word text: *I'm in.*

Getting a ticket for the train the next morning proved more diffi-cult than normal. That was to be expected as thousands of panicked people tried to evacuate the city. Millions more stayed, determined not to give in to the evil men who carried out the attacks.

Once she was in London, she took a cab to the rendezvous location and waited. A black sedan picked her up on the curb where she stood overlooking the River Thames. The driver had been the guard now standing by the door.

Two short knocks came from the other side, rousing her from her thoughts. A second later, the Director walked through, walked around the glass desk before her, and eased into his seat.

A silver laptop sat atop the surface next to a short stack of papers and a single pen.

"I changed my mind," Adriana said.

"I can see that. I suppose that has everything to do with the Paris attacks?"

"A little."

"No cause for false impressions, Adriana. Most unfortunate, the events of the last twenty-four hours. Still, sometimes we must be shaken to truly find our calling."

"I'm not shaken," she said. "I was close to ground zero when it happened. The attack in the 10th Arrondissement was just a few blocks from where I was working."

"On another missing art case?"

"Something like that."

"And how is that coming along?" He had a snide tone to his voice.

"I've dropped it. That's why I'm here. If you want me to leave, though, no problem."

She stood up and turned toward the door.

"No reason to get testy, Miss Villa. I know why you're here. And I appreciate you calling, especially considering the gravity of the situation." He slid the stack of papers across the desk.

"What's that?"

"Asad's dossier along with all his known contacts across Europe. We've marked off the ones that have expired."

"Expired?"

"Died. It happens."

She stepped closer to the desk and picked up the stack. "Shouldn't this be in a folder or something?"

The Director rolled his eyes. "I took the liberty of removing it, but if you like I can get it for you."

She shook her hand as she pored over the contents of the stack. Shadow Cell had been busy, and the Director and his colleagues had managed to compile quite a list of contacts, resources, and other pertinent information on Asad and his associates. She couldn't help wondering: If they had all that intel, why hadn't they just taken him out?

"So, what's the problem?" she asked, returning the stack of papers to the edge of the desk.

"I beg your pardon?"

"You seem to know everything about this guy. Why don't you just send in a special forces group to take him out while he's on the toilet or something?"

"At any given moment, Asad is surrounded by two dozen armed, well-trained guards. And that's just when he's asleep. During the day, he has a small army around him. He's nearly impossible to reach."

She frowned. "Okay. You have bombs, don't you? We've all seen the footage of what the Western air forces can do. Why not bomb him back to the Stone Age?"

The Director sighed. "If his base of operations were somewhere in the middle of the Syrian Desert, that might be a viable option. Unfortunately, his headquarters is here in London. At least as far as we can tell. He runs a series of profitable businesses. They're all legitimate. And every one of them funnels money into the Red Ring."

"And you can't trace it."

"Some of it. Not all. We need you to get to Asad, find out what he knows, and take him out."

She snorted. "Sounds simple enough."

"It's anything but, Adriana."

"If it's so tough, why don't MI5 or MI6 take it on?"

"They passed on the mission."

Her eyebrows lifted.

"June will get you all the details. She'll be your contact on this one. Should you decide to stay on with us, assuming you survive, she will be your point person going forward."

Adriana took a deep breath and sighed. She turned and started to walk out the door.

"Miss Villa?"

She spun around and saw the Director holding the paperwork out to her. "You might need these."

Adriana smirked. "Thank you, Director Hughes. I appreciate it, but I have everything I need."

His forehead wrinkled. "I see June gave you my name."

She shook her head. "Nope. I figured it out."

At the door, she stopped and turned her head, facing the guard. "It was a pleasure talking to you." She opened the door and stepped out.

The guard turned toward Director Hughes and shook his head as if denying any discussion had taken place. He frowned but said nothing.

The door opened again suddenly, and she poked her head in. "Oh, I forgot to ask where I'm supposed to go next."

"Third door on the left. Henry in the armory will get you everything you need."

"Thank you."

She closed the door and started down the corridor. There was an excitement brewing deep down inside her. It was something she felt every time she got started on a lead with a work of art. This time, it was slightly different. There was a greater sense of purpose.

She knew there would be danger ahead, the kind that could mean certain death. That didn't deter her. After what she saw in Paris, Adriana knew that no one was safe, no matter what occupation they chose.

It was time to take the fight to the terrorists. It was time to make them feel fear.

5

LONDON

"Y̲ou guys sure are good at using old abandoned buildings," Adriana said, looking around at the underground laboratory.

The walls were made from old brick that crumbled in more than a few places. The mortar had fallen off in others. Steel girders ran along the roof overhead in dramatic arches, creating several small domes along the length of the room.

"Real estate is cheaper that way," a young man in a black button-up shirt said. He was standing next to a series of steel cabinets that lined the wall. "Name is Henry," he said.

"Adriana," she said, shaking his hand.

"I know who you are."

She let go.

He hurried to correct himself. "I didn't mean that in a creepy way. I just...I've heard about you. It's my job to know who we're bringing in."

"Fair enough. What have you got for me, Henry?"

He blushed at the sound of his name and pushed the black-rimmed glasses up higher on his nose.

A metal briefcase sat atop a glass table, not unlike the one

Director Hughes used for a desk. Henry unlatched it and produced a key fob. "This is for your car. Black Jaguar XE R-Sport."

They do love their new Jags, she thought.

"Does it come with an ejector seat or missiles?"

He chuckled. "No, nothing like that. It's just a really fast car."

She couldn't help but feel just a tad disappointed.

"I know you have your own collection of guns," he said. "However, they had this piece specially made just for you." He lifted a black pistol out of the case and handed it to her.

She raised an eyebrow as she inspected the piece. It was almost exactly like Sean's .40 caliber Springfield. The only difference was a modification made to the barrel.

"We made some adjustments," Henry said, pointing at the barrel. "It produces 25 percent less recoil so you can be more accurate. The downside is—"

"Loss of range. Yes, I get it," she said, cutting him off as she inspected the weapon.

"Yes, right." He looked in the case again and found a suppressor. "This will keep things quiet." He passed it to her.

She screwed it on and held it out at arm's length, closing one eye to look down the sights.

"You'll notice it didn't add much to the front-end weight," he said.

"It really didn't. How did you manage that?"

"That's a secret recipe I'm not at liberty to discuss. Let's just say it involves titanium, shall we?"

She puckered her lips, impressed. "Fair enough."

"Of course, we'll equip you with any other gadgets you may need, tracking devices, that sort of thing. You'll find everything in the boot of your car."

Boot. She loved how the English called the trunk a boot.

"When can I take all this out for a spin?"

"Spin?" He looked surprised. "There's no spin. You start today. I assumed the Director told you that. Did he give you your mission objective, dossier, all that?"

"Yes." She sounded hesitant. "He did. So, I'm not going to go through any orientation or training for all this?"

Henry's head twitched to the side. "Um, you just went through it. Just now. When I was talking to you about the gun and car and gizmos and all that."

"Oh. Seems kind of minimal, don't you think?"

Henry passed her a cute smile. "You'll be fine. You were very highly recommended. If we're to believe all the things June told us about you, I'd say you have nothing to worry about."

Adriana wasn't so sure. She placed the weapon back in the case, closed it, and picked it up. She looked over at Henry. "Show me the car."

The two walked to the end of the vast room and stopped next to a metal rail. A huge space opened up before them with several different vehicles parked in a row, facing toward closed garage doors.

"The black one over there?" Adriana asked, spying the car that had been described earlier. The black sedan had matching wheels and darkly tinted windows. She'd always had an affinity for European cars, especially the German ones. These new Jags, though, were definitely in her wheelhouse.

"That's the one. R-Sport, too. That car will do anything but fly, although it will feel like it can."

Adriana couldn't wait to get behind the wheel. It wasn't her first time. She'd driven that exact model before.

"I told you that we hadn't installed any sort of over-the-top gadgets in that ride," Henry said. "That wasn't entirely true. There are a couple of features that could come in handy under the right circumstances. Look on your key fob."

She held up the tiny black device and examined it.

"That panel on the back will read your thumbprint. The car can't be started without pressing your thumb to that first. It features a remote start system for faster ignition and quicker getaways. However, if you don't put your thumb to that little pad, nothing will happen."

She couldn't hide her disappointment. Adriana had hoped for

something a little sexier, like machine guns that popped out of the headlights or a flamethrower built into the tailpipe.

"Here's the cool part," Henry went on. "If someone other than you or one of our authorized agents tries to use this, the engine will lock down, and your exact position will be relayed to us. Depending on where you are in the world, the authorities will be alerted and will converge on your location."

Her right eyebrow raised. "I suppose you said depending on where I am because there are some countries where you can't call the cavalry."

"There are, admittedly, a few Third World places where it could be more difficult to call in reinforcements, yes. Those places are few and far between."

"Anything else I should know about? Anything at all?"

"That's pretty much it. Sorry, I know. Not all that sexy, is it?"

She rolled her shoulders. "It's okay. The car definitely is."

"Come on," he said. "Time for you to meet with June about your assignment."

Adriana followed Henry away from the railing and down a hall that looked like all the others: old brickwork from the Industrial Age. They hung a right at the end and continued along the corridor until they came to a glass wall separating them from the office on the other side. June was sitting at her desk in front of a laptop when the other two approached.

She motioned them to come in before they could even knock.

"I see you met Henry," June said in a pleasant tone. She was dressed in a white business suit with her golden hair pulled back in a tight ponytail.

"Yes, and he's been very helpful."

"Will you be needing anything else from me?" Henry asked. He stood by the door waiting eagerly.

"No, thank you. We're good."

He gave a nod and glanced at Adriana again. "Good luck, although I doubt you'll need it."

Adriana returned the nod and stepped toward June's desk.

"Please, have a seat." June said, motioning to a modern black chair with shiny metal legs.

Adriana eased into it and crossed one leg over the other. "Okay, so this all seems kind of fast," she said. "I mean, I just got here, and it feels like I'm being sent out immediately."

June smirked. "You are." She stood up and stepped over to a counter with white shelves. A coffeemaker steamed with fresh brew. "Want a cup of coffee?"

"No, thanks. Already had some earlier."

June poured the hot brown liquid into a mug. After setting the pot back on the coffeemaker, she returned to her seat and picked up a small remote control. She took a sip and then pressed a button. The room's lights dimmed, and a projector hanging from the ceiling switched on. It cast a beam of light through the room to the far wall.

A man in a New York Yankees cap and a Chelsea Football Club track jacket was standing on the corner of a street somewhere in London. The entrance to the tube was in the background along with hundreds of people going about their day. Most of them appeared to be coming home from work. At least that was Adriana's assessment.

"This is Youssef. He's a low-level functionary for the Red Ring. For the most part, he takes care of lots of menial tasks: housing, food, clothing, girls, that sort of thing. He provides all of that for the ring's soldiers."

"Soldiers?" Adriana narrowed her eyes.

"They believe themselves to be soldiers in a holy war against the materialistic West. The reality is they're nothing more than terrorists."

"You said girls."

"Yes." June's expression was one of disgust. "They bring in young girls for their soldiers to use. A good amount of the ring's money comes from private funding. It's well laundered and difficult to track. Some of it, however, comes from the child sex trade."

"Human trafficking?" It was Adriana's turn to be disgusted. And it wasn't her first run-in with those kinds of scum.

"Unfortunately, yes. Since the American intervention in the

Middle East, one of the sad parts of the war has been an increase in human trafficking out of that region, not to mention the rampant production of opium. The governments in Afghanistan and Iraq are too preoccupied with the insurgency to worry about some of the other crimes happening right under their noses. The Red Ring knows that, and so they operate without fear."

"So, they believe they're doing the work of God while at the same time selling young women as sex slaves?"

"Yes. And they drug them to keep them docile. It's horrible, which is all the more reason for us to take them down and do it as quickly as possible."

"This guy, Youssef, he got a last name?"

"I'm sure he does, but he just goes by Youssef."

"Like a Brazilian soccer player."

"I guess. We figure that's probably a nickname or one he chose. He's slippery, and despite looking like a pretty ordinary guy he has managed to keep us from getting much on him other than his connections to the ring. His background is sketchy at best. What we can tell you is that he likes young girls and often keeps one or two for himself before sending them off. He also has a penchant for cocaine."

Adriana nodded. Everyone had a vice. This guy had them in spades. It was bothersome that June's organization didn't have much intel on Youssef. Adriana wondered if that was an issue with most terrorist organizations. Getting a name and a face was one thing. Learning about the person's life story was something else. Not that it mattered. As long as they could be found and apprehended, questioned, or eliminated, that was what was important.

"How do I find him?" Adriana asked after a moment of thought.

"He usually hangs out in Chelsea, has a flat there a few blocks from the Thames."

"Nice section of town."

"Indeed. He appreciates the finer things in life. Eats at expensive places. Drives a Maserati and a Porsche."

"Sounds like we need to find out where he's getting his allowance."

"Precisely." June tossed a folder across her desk. "All the info you need on him is in there. I also took the liberty of sending a PDF to your email as well. It's password protected. Seven, eight, two, six, seven, nine. Need me to repeat it?"

Adriana shook her head. "No, I'm good. Anything else I need to know?"

"I don't have to tell you how dangerous this is. Youssef may look like a punk and not wield any power, but make no mistake, he's a ruthless killer. If he catches you, we may not be able to help."

Adriana figured she'd be on her own. According to the Director, there weren't many people working for Shadow Cell to begin with. "I'll watch my back," she said as she stood.

June got out of her seat as well. "Let me know if you need anything. You have my direct line."

Adriana walked over to the door and pushed it open. She started to step back out into the hallway when June stopped her.

"Adriana?"

She turned around and looked across the room at her friend. "Yeah?"

"Thank you."

"For what?"

"Doing this. I know it's dangerous."

Adriana took a long breath and sighed. "Once upon a time, our boyfriends made the conscious decision to use their skills to benefit mankind. I think it's time I do the same."

6

LONDON

Youssef stepped out of the cafe holding what Adriana assumed was a cup of coffee. Maybe it was tea. She didn't really care. All she cared about was the target and getting the information she wanted out of him.

The dossier and mission information June had given her were all she'd needed to find Youssef. That wasn't the problem.

Youssef was hardly elusive. In fact, the guy basically put a spotlight in the air wherever he went so that everyone would know where he was. He shelled out cash across town. He bought clothes, shoes, even flat-brimmed baseball caps. And it was just a Tuesday.

He was careful, though, in his way. He took his bodyguards with him everywhere. While that certainly made getting to him more difficult, he made the mistake of ordering his two men to stay outside in the car or by the doors whenever he went into a store or a shop. And he didn't make the mistake once. It was everywhere the guy went.

Adriana peered through the Jag's windshield, watching the target leave the coffee shop and climb in the back of his Bentley. One guard got in behind the wheel. The other joined their employer in the back.

A few seconds later, they pulled away, and Adriana wheeled her car into traffic behind them. While the Jag was remarkable, it made blending in difficult. The ostentatious black exterior and dark window tinting made the thing reek of official government vehicle.

She kept several cars between her and the mark, just to be safe, but that made tailing Youssef tricky. Dense gray clouds overhead spat rain down onto the city by the Thames. That would make spotting her a little more difficult. That problem was reciprocated on her end, too, and she had trouble keeping an eye on the Bentley.

Youssef's driver wove through the stop-and-go traffic. He made several turns in both directions, which at one point caused Adriana to wonder if she'd been spotted. She could have sworn they'd been down one of the streets before. She shook off the paranoia and kept going. All she could do was keep a small part of the Bentley in view and hope they didn't notice.

The journey wound through the city, passing the center of London along the way. They continued a little farther beyond the middle of town until suddenly Youssef's car turned into a parking spot along the sidewalk in front of a massive, modern-looking building. Shops lined the main floor and wrapped around the huge structure. Adriana immediately recognized where they were. The sleek metal and glass of the One New Change mall was a stark contrast to many of the older buildings in London. Where the city's historic buildings held on to that history, to their piece of British culture, the mall stood out as a bastion of capitalism and modernity.

Adriana scanned the row of cars ahead, praying a spot opened up nearby.

Luckily, someone in a Fiat pulled out several cars ahead. She clenched her teeth in hopes that none of the other vehicles in front of her would take the space. She whipped the car into the parking spot and glanced back in her mirror. The guard from the back seat of Youssef's ride was closing the door. The target was striding hurriedly into the open-air walkway between the two main buildings that composed the sprawling shopping complex.

The driver rushed to keep up, and a moment later the three men disappeared into the corridor.

Adriana cursed herself for watching without moving. She got out of her car and rechecked to make sure her weapon was in place inside the long black jacket she'd donned earlier that day.

English weather, especially that time of year, could turn cold and damp at a moment's notice. To be fair, she'd not experienced a great deal of time in that city when the weather wasn't that way.

She took off at a trot, keeping close to the shops and boutiques along the sidewalk in case one of the guards peeked back around the corner. She was being silly, and she knew it. They hadn't spotted her. Not yet, at least.

Adriana turned the corner where the men had vanished from view and looked into the core of the mall. People milled about in open areas with umbrellas overhead. A few didn't seem to mind the sparse bit of rain and simply stood out in the open. Dozens of stores lined the walkway. Most of them appeared to be pretty high end. For a moment, she'd wondered why someone like Youssef would bother going to a mall, but upon seeing some of the exclusive shops, she understood immediately.

What she didn't know, was where the mark had gone.

Her eyes darted everywhere. She fought a wave of panic, reminding herself that the guy had to be there somewhere.

There. On the other end of the path, she caught a glimpse of Youssef and his guards going into one of the main entrances to the mall.

Adriana took off running. At the moment, there was no need to be concerned about being spotted. The minute she lost sight of the three men going into the building, she'd have a much more difficult time finding them again.

Of course, she could always resume her mission, start over from the beginning tomorrow, but time was critical. Every day this scumbag was on the streets, another girl was being sold into sexual slavery. And another terrorist was getting money to fund their sinister operations.

Adriana had to get him today. There was no other option.

She reached the end of the corridor and rushed through the doors. She scanned the area and found the three men almost to the top of the escalator leading to the second floor. She brushed off some of the loose droplets of rain from her jacket and fixed her hair so she didn't look like she'd just been running in the rain.

The mall's warm air wrapped around her. The rich smells of perfume and leather wafted into her nostrils. It was a cornucopia of the shopping stimuli.

Adriana hurried over to the escalator and stepped on. Youssef and his guards were already getting off at the top. She played it cool, taking a few casual steps up as the steps carried her upward.

She watched as the men strode purposefully around the railing to the next escalator and stepped on.

"Up again," Adriana said to herself. "Where are you going?"

She picked up the pace slightly until she reached the top of the escalator. Around the corner, the men were already on their way up. Adriana navigated around a gaggle of children whose mother was desperately trying to keep them together.

Adriana shoved her hands in her jacket pockets to make sure she still appeared to be nothing more than a casual shopper as she made her way over to the next escalator.

One of Youssef's guards turned his head in her direction. She averted her gaze, twisting her head to look in the jewelry shop to her right. She took a few lazy steps toward the boutique before drifting back the other way toward the escalator. She kept her head forward, but stole a short look up out of the corner of her eye. Youssef and his guards were getting off on the third floor, apparently paying no attention to her.

She sped up again and climbed aboard the escalator, this time taking faster steps toward the top.

Adrenaline coursed through her. There was only one more escalator to go. Were they going to the roof? She wondered why the men hadn't taken one of the elevators if that was the case.

Once more, she watched as they boarded the last escalator and slowly ascended to the top floor. This time, instead of following right behind them, Adriana walked over to a women's clothing store and stepped inside. She wasn't stupid. In her experience, guards like the one with Youssef would have their heads on a swivel. If they noticed the same woman one floor down more than once, they'd be startled like frightened woodland creatures.

She found a spot behind a mannequin wearing a long green dress and peeked out from behind it. Both guards were looking around, making sure nothing suspicious was going on. She'd been correct to find a hiding spot. The problem now was that she was losing ground.

That didn't matter much. The men didn't have anywhere else to go except the stores on the fourth floor, or perhaps the rooftop bar.

She didn't know why, but Adriana had a strange feeling it was the latter.

This time, the men veered to their right and wandered toward the end of the mall and a gray metal door. They were heading for the stairs.

Adriana frowned. The elevator surely would have been quicker. What were they playing at?

"May I help you?" a woman asked in a polite tone.

The question momentarily startled Adriana. She spun around and realized it was just the store's salesperson.

"I really love this color, but I'm going to have to come back later."

She rushed out of the shop and out onto the main walkway. The men disappeared through the door and into the stairwell. Adriana kicked it into high gear, nearly speed walking over to the escalator. She climbed it rapidly, taking the steps two at a time until she reached the top.

When she arrived at the stairwell door, she paused and pressed her fingers to her jacket. She felt the weapon through the fabric. Satisfied it was still in place, she pressed down on the handle's button and eased the door open.

Thankfully, it didn't squeak, which was what she'd feared would happen. She slipped through the opening and looked around inside to make sure the men weren't close.

She heard a door slam shut from the top of the stairs. That was all the confirmation Adriana needed.

She crept upward, making sure her shoes made no sound as she climbed. After rounding the first corner, she checked above, sweeping the area with the pistol in case one of the guards had lingered behind.

As she climbed the remainder of the steps, another thought occurred to her: *What if this is some kind of trap?*

Surely they hadn't seen her. Then again, if Adriana believed someone was following her, she would have taken similar action: skip the elevator, go up a sequence of escalators, then go up the stairs to... she saw the sign next to the door. It read *Roof Access, Authorized Personnel Only.*

Something wasn't right.

Adriana was already reaching for the door handle when she changed her mind.

She pulled back to the corner of the platform and waited with pistol in hand. If it was a trap, walking through the door would be a fatal mistake. These guys weren't the type to let someone go unless it was over a high ledge.

So, she stayed put and waited.

Five minutes went by, and still nothing happened.

She was about to give in and push through the door when she heard a man's deep voice on the other side.

"Must have been a false alarm, sir."

One of the other men, she assumed Youssef, chastised the one who spoke first. She couldn't clearly hear what he was saying, but it didn't sound good.

"I thought she was following us, sir. I apologize."

"Can't believe you wasted my time like this," Youssef said. His voice was much closer than before. He was coming toward the door.

Adriana pressed her back against the wall next to the door's hinges and waited with her weapon held in her right hand close to her cheek.

The door handle jiggled. The sound echoed down through the stairwell. Then it turned, and the door swung open.

"I'm a busy man," Youssef was saying. "I don't have time to run from shadows."

Like a flash of lightning, Adriana's left hand shot out and grabbed Youssef by the shirt. The man was probably an inch or two under six feet and nearly two hundred pounds. By no means was he little, but he wasn't exactly a gym rat, either.

She yanked him to the side and kicked the door closed on the two guards. It was a temporary stop, but it was all she needed to buy enough time to secure her hostage.

When the guards burst through the door, they found their boss with an arm around his throat and a pistol to his head.

They aimed their weapons at her, but she gave almost no target. One wrong twitch and their employer's head would be the one splattered on the wall.

"Let him go," one said.

She recognized it as the apologetic voice from the conversation a minute before.

"I'm going to say no to that," Adriana said. "Put your weapons down, or I kill him right now."

The guards narrowed their eyes, probably wondering what they should do.

"Do what she said, you idiots," Youssef wheezed. He was desperately trying to get enough air into his lungs.

She squeezed tighter, and he clawed at her forearms, struggling to free himself.

The men hesitated. Adriana pressed the muzzle harder against Youssef's temple.

"Do it," she said.

The guard on the left moved first, gradually lowering his weapon toward the floor. The one on the right didn't react as quickly.

"I will kill him and then you," she warned.

"You idiot," Youssef spat through clenched teeth. "Do it or I'll kill you myself."

The man blinked rapidly and then obeyed. He bent down at the waist and put the gun on the floor next to the other.

"That's better," Adriana said. "Now, be good boys, and kick them over here for me."

Again, they hesitated but did as instructed without needing to be told twice this time. The weapons slid on the smooth concrete and stopped at her feet.

"One last request, gentlemen. Get down on your knees for me."

After they'd done as told, she eased her grip on Youssef's throat. He gasped for air the second he felt her forearm loosen.

"Very good. Glad to see you can learn. Now, Youssef, you and I are going to have a little talk."

He snickered. "Talk? About what? How I'm going to have your head for this? Perhaps along with some other parts?"

His English was perfect. His accent was definitely foreign. Which Middle Eastern country, she wasn't sure.

She squeezed his neck tight again. "That isn't very nice. You shouldn't piss off a woman who's holding a gun to your head. Now, tell me about the Red Ring. We know you're planning something big. I want to know what it is."

He let out a laugh, though it was hard to with her arm around his throat. He started to say something, but she squeezed harder.

"Before you say something stupid," she cut him off, "you should know that I have very little patience for cliché answers like you're probably going to give me. You know, the typical 'I'm not saying anything' or 'the Red Ring is more powerful than you'll ever know,' so I recommend just telling me the plan before I make this really painful for you."

He started to snicker.

"See?" she said. "You're laughing. Which means you either don't think I can hurt you, or you're going to give me one of those tired speeches we talked about a second ago."

Youssef tried to swallow, a tough task with Adriana's arm strangling him.

He said something in Arabic to the two guards.

They nodded at the same time.

"Really?" Adriana asked. A thick tone of cynicism carried in her voice. "You just told them to kill me the second I let go? What makes you think I'm going to let go? Oh, and I speak Arabic. Did you honestly think someone in my position wouldn't?"

He did his best to shake his head. "You don't understand. It's already in play. There is nothing you can do to stop it, no matter what I tell you."

"Let's go ahead and try that anyway."

"No. I think instead you're going to die."

Adriana frowned. Something wasn't right. It wasn't just the man's brazen lack of fear. She sensed someone else in the stairwell. Suddenly, Adriana spun around and stepped to the side, releasing her hostage as she moved. Gunfire came from the next level down in a split second, tempered by suppressors on the men's weapons.

Bullets tore through Youssef's body, splattering crimson all over the floor and his two guards.

He shook and gyrated as the rounds riddled his body. The shooting stopped and he wavered for a second. Then he fell forward toward the railing and toppled over. His body tumbled between the stairs. His head hit a railing two floors down and caused the body to spin wildly out of control until it hit the bottom.

The two guards rushed toward their weapons, desperate to take out Adriana. She spun and unleashed a shot into the closest one's head, dropping him instantly. The second she shot in the neck and back.

She spun around and looked down the stairwell at the other two gunmen.

They were gone.

7

LONDON

Adriana ran down the stairs, skipping two or three at a time. She could hear the gunmen hurrying down but only saw a hand now and then as they gripped the railing to brace their descent.

She stopped on the third floor and aimed her weapon down the shaft until she caught a glimpse of an arm. She fired three times, but the rounds ricocheted off the railing and concrete walls.

She cursed herself for missing and started running again.

By the time Adriana reached the second floor, she heard a door slam shut down below. The men had gone outside—or at least that's what they wanted her to think.

She slowed her pace and crept around the corner of the last landing before the main floor. She swept her weapon around the confined space to make sure it was clear. Even then, she stopped and waited in case one of the gunmen was lying in wait to pop open the door and shoot her at point-blank range.

After a few seconds, she rushed to the door and swung it open, poking the gun's barrel through the crack.

Nothing but panicked shoppers filled the mezzanine as they ran for the exits. The shootout in the stairwell must have sent them into hysteria. Adriana saw no sign of the shooters. She closed the door again and sighed. If people were panicking, she'd have to get out of there before the cops arrived.

She sighed in frustration and turned her attention to Youssef's corpse lying a few feet away in a pool of thick red liquid.

She grimaced at the sight of the twisted limbs, at the unbelievable amount of blood.

Adriana had seen her share of dead bodies, some of which she'd put in that permanent state of rest. This one, however, was a little bloodier than usual. Youssef's skull was crushed in on the side. His torso, shoulders, arms, and a few places on his thighs, had been shredded by the mystery shooters' bullets.

Too bad that Youssef couldn't reveal any secrets now.

She checked her magazine, quickly counting how many rounds she had left before sliding it back into place.

A bitter, acrid smell filled the room. Adriana knew the scent: gun smoke and blood.

She stuffed the gun back in its holster in the folds of her jacket and was about to walk out the door when she heard a low but distinct noise—like a hum or a rattle—coming from Youssef's body.

Her head snapped around, and she stared down at the dead man. The sound kept coming. She bent down on one knee. Doing her best to keep out of the blood pooling on the floor, she sifted carefully through the man's clothes until she found the source of the noise.

She pulled his phone out of a pocket and looked at the number on the screen. No way she was going to answer it, no matter how tempting it was.

The call ended and the phone went silent.

Adriana stuffed the device into her left pocket and started for the door. A second after she pushed it open, she saw the swarm of cops charging her way.

She stepped back and let the door close. It was beyond time to leave.

She turned and bounded up the stairs, flung open the second-level door, and rushed through.

Her feet skidded to a stop. Hundreds of panicked shoppers rushed to the escalators, pushing and shoving their way toward the exits.

The phone vibrated again a single time. She knew that meant whoever called probably left a voicemail.

Adriana hurried to remove the phone from her pocket. She was about to hit the listen button when the phone suddenly went dark. She frowned and hit the home button. It brought up a screen saver of the late Youssef surrounded by exotic cars.

The phone was locked, and there wasn't enough time to try to crack the password. Adriana was lucky the device hadn't been damaged in the gunfire or the fall to the floor. With Youssef dead, her only possible link to the Red Ring was that phone. She wondered who had called and left a message.

The device abruptly vibrated again, and the lock screen simply showed the words *text message* on the screen.

Again, she didn't have a way to investigate without the passcode. Hacking electronic devices wasn't her thing. Ancient languages, foreign languages, art history, investigative skills, and general butt-kicking were all part of her repertoire. The digital stuff, however, was not.

Fortunately, another one of Adriana's skills was her ability to network with all sorts of people, including some with less than legitimate backgrounds. One name immediately came to mind.

The guy's real name was Raymond, but everyone in the hacker community knew him as A-Tak. Adriana had given him grief about the nickname, insisting on calling him Ray to the point where she thought he might cry. Apparently, he didn't like his real name—any version of it.

Ray was able to hack pretty much any electronic device. Didn't matter what brand or operating system, he knew how to work it. Phones were a little different, but she didn't have a choice. Ray was her only chance at finding Camir Asad.

Pocketing the device again, Adriana stepped out onto the second floor and stuffed her hands in her pockets to look as casual as possible. She strode toward the escalator amid people running and screaming. A man bumped into her as he recklessly sprinted for the escalator. The bump sent a dull pain through Adriana's shoulder and briefly knocked her off balance. She kept moving toward the escalator, hoping no one would notice her, when a man's voice from behind froze her stiff.

"Miss?" the guy said in a sharp accent. "Hold it right there."

Her eyes blinked rapidly. She didn't know what to expect. Was it a cop? Mall security? She slowly twisted around and realized it was the former.

A man in full uniform was approaching her with what she perceived to be the utmost caution.

"Is there a problem, Officer?" she said. It was a line she'd picked up in the States, although she figured it probably got used internationally.

"That depends," he said as he took another wary step toward her.

She could feel the weapon in her jacket pressing against her side. No way she was going to use it. He was one of the good guys, like her —unless he'd been bought. She shook off the notion.

"Depends?"

He held up a phone in his right hand. "On how much you need this. I saw you drop it when that guy bumped into you a moment ago. Hope it isn't damaged."

He examined it closely, twisting it around in his fingers.

Adriana caught her breath. She hoped there wasn't any blood on it. She'd never really checked for that, although if there had been it might have rubbed off in her jacket. Either way, if he saw anything suspicious, getting out of the mall would be a much trickier proposal.

"Looks like it's all right. Might want to hold on to it, though. Doesn't seem very secure in your pocket."

She stepped toward him and put on the best appreciative smile she could muster. "Thank you so much, Officer. I appreciate it." She took the device and had a quick look to make sure it wasn't cracked. The cop didn't need to know that all she cared about was what information the phone contained. At this point, it was all about appearing to be nothing more than a confused shopper.

"I heard someone say there were gunshots," Adriana said. She put on her victim face.

"We're not sure what it was, Miss. We just know we're trying to get people out of here as fast as we can to make sure everyone is safe."

His canned response was standard operating procedure. The authorities wouldn't give away details because of the panic it could incite. From the looks of things, it wasn't working. People were freaking out.

"Thank you," she said.

"Best be going. Careful getting out."

"Yes, sir."

The man turned and strode away, waving other shoppers toward the exits.

Adriana didn't push her luck. She trotted over to the escalator and after waiting a moment stepped on and didn't look back.

At the bottom, dozens more officers were ushering people out the doors. They were doing their best to maintain some kind of order, but the entire scene was chaotic.

Adriana blended in with the masses and let the momentum of the group carry her to the doorway. Out of the corner of her eye she saw the British version of a SWAT team enter the building off to the right through a maintenance door. Instinctively, she lowered her head as she passed through the exit and out into the rainy London day.

More police were outside, hurriedly corralling people away from the building. She followed the group for a moment and then made a sharp right. It didn't take long for her to reach her car. Getting out of the area, on the other hand, took a great deal of patience. She waited in the thick traffic for nearly half an hour until she was finally able to get clear of the mayhem.

Once the mall was out of sight, she breathed a sigh of relief.

She imagined the cops finding the dead bodies in the stairwell and wondered what they'd piece together from the crime scene. More than that, she was curious about the two shooters who'd managed to escape. Clearly, they weren't Youssef's men. So, who were they? Why'd they show up when they did? The more she thought about it, the more Adriana came to one conclusion: Someone else had targeted Youssef. It was the only explanation.

She pieced together the facts in her head.

The men showed up shortly after she did. According to the conversation with his men, Youssef's guards believed they were being followed. That meant they might have called for backup. The plausibility of that argument vanished when the new gunmen blew away Youssef.

If they were there to help, it was highly unlikely they'd have been so free with the triggers.

No, the more Adriana thought about it, the more she believed someone else had targeted Youssef.

Then there was the matter of the phone call and text message he'd received immediately after being killed. Was it the person responsible for the hit?

There was only one way to find out.

8

LONDON

Adriana rapped on the door again and took a step back. She waited for nearly a minute before she knocked again, this time with more fervor.

"Open up, Ray. I know you're in there," she said with her face pressed close to the door.

Ray lived in Holloway, an inner-city section of town. He rented a small townhouse in a rundown neighborhood where prices were low and so were the expectations. It wasn't that Ray didn't have money. As far as Adriana knew, the guy was loaded. He could have easily afforded much more luxurious accommodations. She guessed he didn't go for that because he wanted to keep up the appearance of being poor, which would help mask what he did for money.

He was eccentric like that.

The sound of three locks being undone preceded the door cracking just wide enough for the man inside to peek through the sliver.

"What do you want?" he asked. He sounded like he'd just woken up.

"Were you asleep? It's three in the afternoon."

"I work late hours. What are you doing here?"

"I need your help," she said. Her head turned side to side. She'd been on full alert since leaving the mall and wouldn't feel safe until she was out of the open. Even then, she probably wouldn't feel *that* safe.

"The last time you needed my help, I nearly ended up dead."

"I know and I'm sorry, but you made money. A lot of money."

"Loads of cash don't do you much good if you're dead."

She sighed. "I know. Look, I'm working on something important. I can't tell you what it is, but I can't do it without you. You're the best hacker in the city."

"Pfft. City. I'm the best in the country, probably on the continent."

"Right. Which is why I'm here." She held up the phone so he could see it.

"Please. If you don't help me find out what's on this, a lot of innocent people could die."

He hesitated for a second, and then the door closed. Adriana was about to knock on it again when she heard a deadbolt slide free once more, then a chain get unhinged, and then two more deadbolts.

Finally, the door swung open. Ray stood on the other side with eyes narrow like slits and pale skin that looked like it hadn't seen the sun in a decade. He was skinny and short, an inch or two shorter than Adriana. Veins popped on his arms and neck showing that, while he was certainly not a big guy, he did have some muscles. Adriana remembered him claiming to be wiry, though she wasn't sure how useful he'd be in a fight.

"What is it?" he asked, staring at the device in her hand.

"Um...it's a phone, Ray."

"Okay, first of all, I know it's a phone. Second, don't call me that. You know I don't like my name."

"Yeah, but are you really going to make me call you by that silly hacker nickname you came up with?"

"You know what? I think we're closed. Thanks for stopping by."

He started to close the door in her face. Adriana reached out and stopped it with her palm.

"Okay, fine. A...Tak. I need to find out what's on this phone. The voice mails, texts, contacts, all of it. I can't get into it because it's password protected."

He peered out of the dark home at her with a dubious expression. "That doesn't sound like your usual sort of request. Who does it belong to? Old boyfriend? High-ranking government official? No, you know, I'm gonna go with boyfriend. You have that crazy look in your eye, like you found out he was sleeping with someone when you were together and now you want revenge. That about right?"

She shoved the door open. The force knocked him back a few steps. She walked into the house and closed the door behind her.

"No. Not even close. This phone belonged to a guy who had connections to known terrorists. I'm trying to find out who and what he knows and what they're planning."

The smart-aleck grin on Ray's face turned sour. "Whoa, wait a minute. Are you working for some government...thing?"

"It's probably better that you don't know. Look, can you crack the phone or not?"

He snorted and stepped around her to lock the door. "Can I crack it? Please. Of course I can, but what's in it for me? Last thing I need is some government suits breathing down my neck for hacking into people's phones." His eyes wandered to the device again. "Who did you say that belonged to?"

"I didn't. And he's dead, so don't worry about it."

Ray's eyes widened. "Dead? You killed him?"

She shook her head. "No, I didn't kill him. He was murdered."

Her host suddenly looked terrified. "And you thought it would be a good idea to come here? I don't know about you, but I like not being dead." He pulled back the curtains and looked out through a window near the door. "Were you followed?"

"No, Ray...I mean, no. You know what, that's a stupid nickname. Everyone else may like it, but I'm not calling you that. I wasn't followed. And as to what's in it for you, money; Ray. I will pay you. That sound good? Of course, maybe you're too scared to try it. Sounds like someone is losing their touch. Perhaps you're not the hacker I thought you were."

Adriana stepped toward the door and started unlocking the deadbolts.

"Now, hold on a second," he said, stepping in front of her. "How much money?"

Ray could always be bought for the right price. It was something Adriana had known since the first time they met.

"Why do you care? You don't buy anything, at least not from the looks of this place."

He let out another short laugh. "I have bills to pay, needs to be met. That's none of your concern. What *is* your concern is how much you're going to pay me to get into that little device."

She reached in her jacket and produced a stack of bills wrapped in a rubber band. "This should get you started," she said. "And finished."

"How much is that?" he asked, taking the stack of money.

"Count it later if you want. I don't care. It's more than you'll make in a year."

"I do pretty well, thank you very much."

She handed him the phone. "Get me into this, and there might be more where that came from."

He glanced down at the device and then back up into her eyes. "Let's have a look then, shall we?"

A minute later, Ray was sitting at a cluttered workstation in the back corner of what Adriana assumed was a living room. An old couch was buried underneath a stack of empty pizza boxes, newspapers, software containers, and a bunch of other junk.

"With the money I'm paying you, you could get a maid to clean up this place," she said with disdain.

"I'm not getting a maid." He reached into a bin that had a pile of wires and other gizmos in it. He removed a little gadget with a wire connected to it and plugged it into the phone, then stuck the other end into a USB port on his laptop. He swiveled his chair a few inches to the right and then started typing away on his computer.

"A lot of people out there do this manually. I came up with a little backdoor program that does all the hard work for me while I sit back and let it unlock the phone."

Adriana knew Ray was a master programmer at heart. He'd received job offers from several major tech companies, some Israeli, a couple based in California. He turned all of them down. Claimed he didn't want to work for "the man," whatever that meant.

Adriana had a sneaking suspicion the real reason was that he made way more under the table than he'd ever make from a legitimate salary.

"Seriously?" She took a look around the room again. "You really live like this? It's a mess."

"Hey, it's my place. I do with it what I like. Okay?"

"Fair enough. Just wondering how girls react when you bring them back here."

He grew uncomfortably quiet for a moment. "Yeah, I don't really meet anyone. Kind of difficult when you're always working and don't leave the house much."

"Aww," she said in a mocking tone. "How sad."

"Hey, I choose it. Besides, I'm saving up."

Her eyebrows raised. "Really? For what?"

"Obviously a better place, but I have plans. I'm not going to stay in this hole forever."

"So, where you thinking of going? Somewhere sunny, I hope."

"Maybe. There will probably be a beach there. Honestly, I just want to find some place warm where there aren't many people around. Then I can kick back and relax without anyone bothering me."

"You want to be a hermit."

"Kind of. I prefer to be left alone. Is that a crime?"

"No," she said. Her mind was thinking that a bunch of the other stuff he did in life probably was. "Just promise me when you eventually get to that place you're talking about that you will hire a maid."

He chuckled. "I may consider it at that point."

The computer dinged and blinked the words *access granted* on the screen.

The phone vibrated, and suddenly the home screen appeared with its many colorful apps.

"And we're in," he declared.

He picked up the phone and handed it to her.

"That didn't take long," she said. There was no effort to mask her surprise.

"Like you said, I'm the best."

"That I did."

She tapped on one of the message threads and read through it.

We need customs officials taken care of at Felixstowe Port. Bartolo must not be detained. See to it our associates are not delayed. Dock 37. This mission is of vital importance. The spear will plunge into the heart of the infidels.

"That's kind of ominous," Ray said after reading the message.

"Spear?" Adriana said to herself. "Bartolo? Who is Bartolo?"

Ray rolled his shoulders. "I don't know. That's your thing. My thing is getting you into *that* thing, remember?"

She nodded absently. The text message read like a strange code. She doubted it was anything like that, but that didn't change the odd way the messenger had worded things.

"Felixstowe Port," Adriana said. "What is that?"

Ray looked surprised. "I thought you were well traveled." After a chastising glare, he decided not to press the issue. "Felixstowe is a major port. It's probably the port for the UK. Couldn't tell you how many ships come in to that place every day, but it's a lot."

He spun around to his computer and tapped the keys rapidly. When he hit enter, a number of images popped up on the screen. "See?" he asked, pointing at the pictures.

"Okay, so Felixstowe is a port. That means the terrorists are picking something up on a ship there."

"The spear?"

She nodded. "Could be. Based on this message, it sounds like they're planning something huge. And what do terrorists do?"

"Cause terrorism?"

"Right, though this sounds bigger than their usual random bombing."

"You don't think it's nuclear, do you?" he sounded hopeful that the answer would be no.

Adriana shrugged. "I don't know. I hope not."

She thought for a second and then tapped the screen. "I need to know how to get there."

"To Felixstowe Port? What are you going to do? You think you can just walk in there and take down a bunch of terrorists? We need to contact the authorities."

She looked at him like his head was on fire. "You? Contact the authorities?"

"I know. Probably the only time I'll ever say that. Still, this sounds dangerous. You need to let the professionals know about this and let them handle it."

Her eyes narrowed. She gazed at the map. "I am the professionals."

9

FELIXSTOWE PORT, ENGLAND

Crates were stacked high in seemingly endless rows along the wharf. Forklifts, cranes, and other huge machines worked tirelessly, moving one container and then another in a constant, repetitive dance. The work was slow, and Adriana knew the moment the dockworkers finished loading one ship, another would be sailing in to take its place and the dance would start all over again.

She remained hidden in the shadows of an old storage building, watching from a distance. A sign close to the gate told her it was Dock 37. According to the message, she was in the right place.

There was no sign of anyone who remotely looked like Asad. In fact, there was no sign of anyone other than the dockworkers who'd been busily working for the last two hours since she arrived.

Adriana didn't consider herself to be an extremely patient person, so it was frustrating after the first hour when Asad and his cronies didn't make an appearance. The text message had been clear enough. She was in the right place.

What if Asad and his men had gotten spooked?

Adriana had made sure Youssef's phone wouldn't automatically lock anymore, which allowed her to respond to the initial message.

She'd thought it prudent to do so. Otherwise, the guy might start to wonder what happened to his associate. If he learned about Youssef's death, however, that would be enough to keep him away if Asad was a particularly excitable type.

Men in his position were usually pretty paranoid. It was how they survived and how they avoided getting into trouble with anti-terrorist agents; agents like her.

She swept the area again with a pair of binoculars. Nothing.

The sun was setting in the west, and the air grew chillier by the minute. Adriana pulled her jacket tight around her arms. Fortunately, the rain had passed through and most of the clouds were to the north. As the hour grew late, the workers on the docks began clocking out and heading home for the day, leaving her pretty much alone.

She let out a long sigh and lowered the binoculars. It was starting to look like her suspicions may have been correct about Asad learning about Youssef's death. Her mind started running with theories.

What if Asad was the one who sent the other two gunmen to take out Youssef? If that was the case and she'd been seen, they might have relayed that information to Asad.

Then there was the issue of her replying to Asad's messages. If he'd ordered the hit on Youssef and his men told him the job was done, a reply after the fact would be a huge red flag for Asad. He'd probably disappear and never resurface. Then again, why would Asad text a guy he'd ordered to be executed? The thoughts swirled in her head like pretzel dough, twisting and confusing her until she decided to refocus on the moment.

That only lasted until she started considering the possibility that Asad wasn't coming.

Adriana cursed herself for potentially botching the mission, although it wasn't her fault. She had no way of knowing the two gunmen were going to show up and take out her target.

The phone in her left jacket pocket vibrated once. It was Youssef's phone.

Asad had sent a message.

Two minutes.

That was it. Nothing else.

She assumed that to mean Asad would be arriving in two minutes. Her impatience gave way to a small dose of panic.

Adriana raised the binoculars again and started sweeping the docks. This time, as she was checking out the area, she noticed something she hadn't before. Between two enormous shipping vessels was a smaller one. It was a merchant ship, probably a tenth the size of the other big boats surrounding it. The containers loaded in the middle just in front of the bridge were also much smaller than the big steel containers lining the docks and stacked on the massive ships. They were wooden, too, which was a distinct difference from the rest of the cargo.

But the most important detail of all wasn't the cargo or the men standing around the edge of the boat's deck, apparently guarding it. The most notable detail was the name of the ship: *Bartolo.*

"How did I miss that?" she asked herself.

Suddenly, a pair of headlights appeared to the left. The SUV rumbled down the asphalt toward the *Bartolo.* Two more SUVs just like it appeared directly behind. The convoy, it seemed, had arrived.

She hopped down from her position between two shipping containers and hurried around the corner. She kept low, crouching as she moved to stay out of sight. At the docks, Adriana attached the suppressor to the muzzle of her weapon to keep things as quiet as possible if it came down to shooting.

She hoped that wouldn't be the case. That desire only grew as she crept around another steel container and saw the men climbing out of the vehicles. There were twelve of them in total, along with Asad, who was wearing a pair of aviator sunglasses and a black jacket and pants.

The other eleven men carried their submachine guns slung over their shoulders. Asad, on the other hand, had no weapon in sight. That meant he was probably carrying a pistol or two underneath his jacket. A man like him was almost always armed. Of that, Adriana was certain.

She watched as Asad waved his finger around. The men immediately trotted through the maze, checking the area to make sure it was clear. Two men stayed close to him while the others finished their routine and then reported back to Asad.

When he appeared satisfied that the location was secure, they started toward the ship.

Adriana crept forward from her hiding spot, moving quickly on her toes to stay as silent as possible. She reached the next container and slipped around the side to the front corner. Another steel box was in her line of sight, so she snuck to the back of it and looked around the edge.

A man emerged from the cabin of the *Bartolo* wearing a dirty cap, a thick navy-blue coat, and a pair of dirty jeans.

Adriana reached into her bag and pulled out a long-range microphone and pointed it at the ship, doing her best to stay in the shadows to avoid detection. She put an earpiece in her right ear and switched on the device.

"Glad you made it safely," the ship's captain said.

It was a safe assumption to think the guy was the captain, although Adriana figured it didn't matter. He wasn't the target.

Asad blew off the captain's greeting. "Where is it?"

The captain cleared his throat, suddenly uneasy. He jerked his thumb toward the cargo on the boat. "It's...it's right over here."

"Show me."

This guy's not much for cordial social conventions, Adriana thought.

Adriana raised her binoculars with her free hand and pressed them against her eyes. She watched through the light from a post near the ship as the men climbed aboard and made their way to the center of the deck. Unlike the giants on either end of it, the *Bartolo* looked more like a tugboat that had been converted to a trade vessel. It was only fifty feet in length, and the roof of the cabin topped out around fifteen feet high. It was clear from first glance that this ship was accustomed to smuggling illegal goods.

The captain stopped at the stack of crates in the middle of the ship and motioned to one of his men who'd been standing next to the cabin door. The guy, perhaps the first mate, hurried over to the box with a crowbar.

"Open it," the captain ordered.

The man obeyed and started prying the lid off the wooden box. It took some work and he had to shift the crowbar from one end to the other, but eventually the top came free.

Asad motioned to two of his men, who immediately shoved the first mate aside. They lifted the crate's lid and stared into the box. Asad slowly removed his sunglasses and leaned closer. He stuck his hand inside and ran it along something. From her point of view, Adriana couldn't see what it was.

"You have fifty of these?" Asad asked.

"Yes, just like you requested," the captain said. His voice trembled. "CX270s. These are the most advanced, most devastating long-range missiles in the world. They fly close to the surface to avoid most radar detection. And missiles like the Patriot and others won't be effective against these."

"Yes, I know the details about this weapon," Asad said. "That's why I requested them. They're the most powerful non-nuclear warhead on the planet. The blast radius is over a kilometer. And the resulting fallout from the chemical warheads we attach, the long-term results will be catastrophic."

"You'll do as you promised? Yes?" the captain asked. "My family. They'll be spared?"

"Of course they will."

"And my payment?"

"In full." Asad reached into his jacket and drew a pistol. He fired a round into the captain's forehead, spraying a pink mist into the light.

Adriana flinched at the sudden execution. The first mate turned to run, but Asad fired a bullet into the man's spine. The guy dropped to the deck, disappearing from Adriana's view. He never got back up.

Asad nodded to one of his men, who raised a radio and spoke a few quick words into it that Adriana couldn't hear.

She frowned and watched as the guards dragged the two bodies over to the starboard side of the ship. They worked quickly, tying the arms and legs to whatever heavy objects they could find on the bridge and on the deck, then dumped the corpses over the side. Two splashes, and the bodies were gone.

A moment later, Adriana heard the rumble of a truck from her left. She turned in time to see the beams from headlights coming around the corner of a building. She dove around the other side of the shipping container, barely avoiding being seen as a cargo truck appeared on the causeway.

The driver cut the lights so as not to draw attention before pulling up next to the ship. He whipped the truck around and backed in to make loading easier for the men aboard.

Adriana rushed around to the front right edge of the shipping container she'd been using for cover. Asad's men started loading the crates, carrying them up the ramp one by one. It took four men per box, which wasn't surprising. Adriana didn't know much about missiles, but she knew they were heavy.

Her pace quickened. She had to do something. If those crates got out of the shipyard, they'd become an immediate threat and she had no way of knowing the targets.

Adriana scanned the ship but saw nothing that could help her cause. Her desperation escalated. They'd already loaded a dozen crates.

She searched the docks and found nothing helpful, not at first.

She spun around and continued the search until she spotted a forklift a hundred feet away parked next to one of the storage buildings. Several spare propane tanks sat next to the wall.

That was it.

Adriana gave a quick look back at the ship. The men were still busily loading the crates. She'd lost count of how many were on the truck. That wasn't going to matter if she could disable it.

She ran on her toes between the stacks of shipping containers and skidded to a halt next to the forklift. She checked the ignition, but there was no sign of the keys. Her first instinct was to check under the seat. Luckily, the last person to drive it had thought the same way she did and stuffed them into a little compartment underneath.

She shoved the key into the ignition and started the engine. She was relieved to hear that the natural gas-powered motor was much quieter than expected.

Adriana hauled one of the spare tanks over to an empty pallet and set it on top. She repeated the process until there were four gas tanks propped on the wooden platform. Then she grabbed some rope sitting nearby and lashed the tanks together to keep them balanced.

She climbed into the seat and analyzed the controls. It took a minute to get her bearings. She flipped a switch and pulled a lever. The forks lifted off the ground. She stopped the movement when the pallet was a few feet high and then spun the wheel.

Adriana took a deep breath and spun the forklift around. She guided it down the path between the steel containers and got ready. The second the men on the ship saw her coming toward them they would likely open fire. She'd have to make sure the machine was lined up perfectly.

She turned the corner and saw the cargo ship and the transport truck. Carefully, she straightened the forklift, aiming it straight at the truck as she stepped on the gas. The machine wasn't fast, but it would do the trick.

She jumped out of the forklift and rolled to the side between two big containers. Then she sprinted down the line, staying just in front of the forklift. Timing was of the utmost importance.

The men on the boat started shouting. But they didn't fire their weapons.

Even better.

She made it back to her previous hiding spot next to the closest container to the boat and looked out. The forklift roared by, closing in on the truck.

The men finally opened fire, but it was too close now.

The truck's engine roared, and suddenly there was a loud bang from the ramp dropping to the ground as the driver pulled the truck away from the dock and sped away toward the exit, narrowly steering clear of the runaway forklift.

She hadn't anticipated that. She'd forgotten the driver still being in the truck. Huge mistake.

The forklift rumbled toward the men firing their guns, but their weapons were built for short-range, and the rounds loosed from their magazines flew wildly past the target.

Adriana poked her head around the container and had to make a decision. Go after the truck or take down Asad and his men. Either way would be a win/lose scenario. There was no way to know how many of the missiles were already on the truck as it sped away toward the exit.

Based on the time it took to load them, she knew there were still several on the ship, as was the target: Asad.

Decision made, Adriana forgot the truck and worked her way around the other side of the shipping container until she reached the front right corner. The repeating pops of gunfire filled the air. She knew what would come next.

As the forklift closed in on the ship, one of Asad's men hit the explosive cargo on the pallet.

One of the tanks ruptured and started spewing gas out of the hole. The thing didn't explode, which surprised her for a second.

The shooting ceased, and men's voices echoed through the ship-yard as they shouted orders to abandon the ship or take cover. Some of the men dove to the other side of the ship for safety. Others jumped back onto land and ran to either side as the forklift plowed into the port side of the ship, digging the sharp metal prongs into the hull. The cluster of fuel tanks slid over the gunwale and onto the deck, leaving one sticking up atop the others.

The boat shuddered. It strained against the moorings as it rocked back and forth. The men who stayed on board, including Asad, stood up and dusted themselves off. They eyed the forklift with cautious curiosity, probably wondering what in the world it was doing there and where the operator went.

Adriana was only thirty feet away, well within her weapon's

range. Just to be safe, she removed the suppressor to help with accuracy and took aim at the tank poking up over the side of the ship. She waited, watching the men approach the wreckage. Asad was already issuing orders and pointing at the fuel tanks. The men who'd jumped ship hurried over to the forklift and shut off the motor.

Now was her chance.

Adriana squeezed the trigger. The bullet struck the gas tank before the men could turn their heads to see where the shot came from. It ripped a hole in the metal, and propane immediately spewed out in a white mist.

The men ducked for cover as she fired again. This time, the spark from hitting the tank did the trick. The tank exploded in a fiery orange ball. Then the others ignited one after the other in a massive display of flaming destruction.

The boat's hull was engulfed in huge fireballs that rolled up into the sky and turned to black smoke. The flames roared across the deck, scorching the crates and setting them alight within seconds.

Adriana didn't watch. Based on what she'd heard about the missiles, she knew she had to get as far away as possible.

She ran hard toward the nearest concrete building she could find, which was back where she'd found the forklift. She reached the door and found it locked. Two quick bullets through the lock fixed that problem, and she dove inside the dark space.

Another explosion rocked the shipyard.

She found another forklift inside. This one was missing its wheels. She crouched up against it, bracing for a big bang. After several minutes, she started to relax.

"The warheads weren't armed," she thought. That was why no big boom had come.

She cautiously stepped over to the door and peeked out.

The *Bartolo* was completely engulfed in a raging fire. She could hear the first signs of sirens, but they were still far away.

She left the building and started running back toward her car. Asad was dead. That would be a problem. He was the last connection. Adriana made a quick decision, and now she worried it was the wrong one.

Asad was their only connection to the rest of the Red Ring. Without him, finding the next person in the chain would be much more difficult.

Unless she could find the truck. She stopped and looked down the path toward the exit where the truck had disappeared a few minutes before.

That was her only chance.

10

_____

LONDON

Adriana slumped down on the bed in her hotel. It was nearly midnight, and she was exhausted. She still had the smell of smoke on her clothes. She sighed and ran her fingers through her tangled hair.

She'd spent hours trying to locate the truck, but she may as well have been trying to find a nickel in the Atlantic Ocean. The vehicle was gone, and there was no way she could find it.

She'd failed. And now there were at least a few dozen dangerous warheads floating around the UK.

How many innocent lives would be lost because of her incompetence? She retraced everything leading up to her decision to join Shadow Cell. She'd thought she could make a difference, save lives. Now people were going to die because of her. Sure, the terrorists had fewer missiles than they wanted, maybe as little as half. That meant half the targets. As much as she wanted to look at it as a glass-half-full scenario, she couldn't.

She laid her head back on the mattress and sighed.

There was nothing Adriana could do. She'd have to report to June that Asad and his men were dead but the truck's driver managed to get away with—what had the ship captain called them?

She propped herself up on the bed and looked over at the gear bag she'd set on the desk in the corner. A second later she was hovering over it, pulling out the device she'd used to record Asad's conversation. It only took a few seconds to rewind it. As she listened to the recording, she heard what the captain had called the missiles.

CX270s.

She flipped open her laptop, and when it connected to the Wi-Fi she entered a search for the same name.

Images of the long-range weapons appeared on the screen along with several results. She clicked on the first one and started reading.

The CX270s were long, slender missiles and looked more like air-to-air weapons she'd seen fixed on jet fighters in the past. They weren't ICBMs, which were much larger and required silos or massive storage facilities. By contrast, the CX270 couldn't cover thousands of miles, but it could cover hundreds. According to the information on the web page, it worked by detonating over the target and dropping hundreds of smaller, powerful explosives down from above.

She noticed a video of some test footage and clicked the play button. Her eyes grew wide as she watched the missile launch from a portable unit somewhere in the desert. It soared into the sky and then popped over a small ridge. Dozens of warheads streaked down through the air. A moment later, the mountain exploded in an enormous plume of fire, smoke, and debris.

"Whoa," she muttered.

The guilt in her chest grew.

Adriana had to find that truck no matter the cost. She'd exhaust every connection she had, scour the earth until she tracked it down.

A vibrating interrupted her thoughts. It was muffled and low, coming from the other room. She glanced over and remembered she'd left her phone in her jacket pocket.

The second she picked up the jacket, she realized it wasn't her phone. It was Youssef's. She still had it.

She looked at the number. It was Asad or at least the number he'd used before.

The call brought a rush of new thoughts to her head. How had he survived the explosion and fire at the docks? She'd seen him a moment before the propane tanks blew.

The only thing Adriana could figure was that he'd been thrown clear of the fire by the blast. Maybe he dove into the water at the last second. Either way, it was Asad's phone calling Youssef's.

The buzzing stopped. Adriana stared at it for a minute, waiting to see what would happen next. As she expected, the device vibrated once. The screen displayed a new voice mail was waiting for her.

She hit the listen button on the screen and put the device to her ear.

It was Asad.

"I find it troubling that on an evening when you failed to meet at our rendezvous that we came under attack. You and I go back a long ways, Youssef. Because of our friendship and your past loyalty to our cause, I will give you one chance to explain yourself. Meet me at the Imperial in one hour. Otherwise, I will hunt you down and kill you myself."

The voice mail ended.

Adriana looked down at the screen and then set the device on the desk. "So, he *is* alive," she said to herself. Under the circumstances, her heart filled with hope again. If Asad was alive, he might have the rest of the missiles.

The second reason for hope was that Asad apparently believed Youssef was still alive. From the sound of it, Asad must have thought Youssef was responsible for the attack at the shipyard.

She picked up the phone and stared at it. If she didn't respond, Asad might get spooked or he might just disappear. She had to keep him on the line. She tapped away at the keyboard and hit send.

I'll be there in 45 minutes.

She set the phone down again and waited to see if he would respond. After a few minutes, she figured no message was coming.

Adriana slid into the desk chair and entered a search for the Imperial. The results populated on the screen, and she picked the first one. The waypoint appeared on the map along with reviews, directions, and hours.

The Imperial was a late-night tea and hookah bar, open until 3 o'clock in the morning. She was glad to see it was only about fifteen minutes away.

That meant she could stake out the place before Asad would be expecting her—or rather, Youssef.

She stuffed her gear back in the rucksack and slung it over her shoulder. Her fatigue disappeared under a surge of adrenaline. The mission wasn't over yet. She still had a chance to reel in the missiles and get Asad.

She'd been lucky.

Now it was time to make her own luck.

Adriana rushed out the door and down the elevator.

She stepped into the lobby and started for the door when she saw two figures coming her way. The men were wearing scarves on their heads and faces, revealing only their dark, sinister eyes.

"Can I help you?" the concierge asked from behind his desk.

The man on the right swung his right arm around and pointed a long pistol at the guy. The gunman squeezed the trigger without saying a word. The bullet plowed through the hotel worker's head.

Adriana instantly cut to her left and around a corner leading into the first-floor hallway.

The second gunman raised his weapon and opened fire. Hot rounds crashed into the corner, narrowly missing her head. She didn't see the drywall exploding behind her as she sprinted down the corridor.

She didn't look back until she'd nearly reached the exit. The first gunman appeared and shot again.

Adriana instinctively dipped her head and barged through the door as a round pierced the glass and sent a spiderweb crack across the panel.

She ducked around the corner behind a white van and laid in wait, holding her weapon on the hood. She kept her sights trained on the door for several minutes, but no one came through.

Then she had a terrifying thought.

She spun around and wiggled through the narrow opening

between the hood of the next car and the wall. Crouching between the vehicles, she crept around to the car's rear and pressed her palms to the wet pavement. Next, she lowered her body so she could see under all the vehicles in the row.

Adriana watched patiently for a moment. She didn't have to wait long. Rushed footsteps sounded from around the corner of the building. Whoever was coming was definitely in a hurry, and there was more than one of them.

Seconds later, two pairs of boots came around the corner. They matched the ones worn by the gunmen. Adriana waited and watched as the two men kept going until they were out in the middle of the parking lot. They slowed to a stop. From the movement of their feet, she could tell they were looking around even though she couldn't see their faces.

"Where did she go?" one of them asked in Arabic.

"I don't know. I told you it was a stupid idea to try to flank her. Now she's gone."

The initial speaker ignored the barb. "Check down that side street. I'll run back around front."

The second guy didn't say anything. Instead, he took off running in the direction his partner suggested. The first guy lingered for another few seconds, probably looking around to make extra certain their target wasn't still there. Then he took off and ran back around the building.

Adriana slowed her breathing. Her car was across the aisle, two rows over. She had to make a break for it, and there wasn't going to be a better time.

She sprang from the damp asphalt and pumped her legs as hard as she could. She kept on her toes to keep silent. The car wasn't far away, maybe thirty feet. She veered toward it while keeping an eye on the alley where the second gunman had run.

She already had the key fob in her hand as she turned into the row and ducked down. The lights blinked when she pressed the button. If either gunman were still around, they would have seen the sudden flashing. She slipped into the driver's seat and revved the engine.

When she whipped the car out of its space, she checked the rearview mirror and saw the gunman in the alley running back toward her. His body appeared and disappeared as he ran through light and then shadow of the parking garage. His weapon was raised, but she knew he was too far out of range.

Adriana gunned the throttle. All four tires gripped the wet pavement and yanked the sedan out of the lot just as the gunman unleashed a flurry of shots.

She looked back as she sped down the street. No one was following her.

She sighed a quick breath of relief and turned at the next corner, disappearing from the scene.

There was no time to wonder who those gunmen were or why they were after her. She'd wondered why they'd killed Youssef before, but that question would have to wait. She glanced at the clock on the car's dashboard. Still plenty of time to find the Imperial.

Adriana had a date with a terrorist, and she had no intentions of missing it.

11

LONDON

Adriana had been to Soho in London once or twice before. It was a hip area with a wide variety of places to eat or grab a drink. Pubs, pizza shops, tea houses, cafes, and even a few coffee joints lined the streets.

The Imperial was one of the few that was still open when she arrived.

Dozens of people loitered around the tea house for a late-night sip. Most of them probably hoped the drink would sober them up after too many hours at the pubs or dance clubs.

One of the pizza parlors was open as well, probably providing the same sobering hope to several other inebriated patrons.

Adriana parked her car a block away and out of sight behind one of the many high-end businesses that occupied the district. The last thing she wanted to do was draw attention.

She approached the Imperial from the north and walked down the sidewalk with her jacket pulled up against her face, both to shield her skin from the cold and from view of potential threats.

As far as she knew, Camir Asad didn't know who she was. The only way he could have was if he'd seen her at the shipyard. His attention, however, had been focused on the forklift barreling toward him and the boat.

Adriana forced herself to push away the questions about how he might have survived the explosion. She'd addressed those already. Now it was more curiosity than anything else, and it wasn't helpful. She had to focus on the present.

She saw the tea house across the plaza and cut over the street to the opposite sidewalk. The concrete path wrapped around a small square with grass in the center and trees planted at each corner. Four park benches were positioned perfectly on each side at the edge of the grass. It was a place where Londoners took their dogs for a walk after the work day ended.

A young couple embraced on one of the benches, locked in each other's gaze. Their breath came out in white puffs of mist in the cold, damp air.

Down a peripheral street, Adriana noted a silver sedan parked at the back of a restaurant. Her eyes diverted to another one of the inlet streets. She immediately recognized one of the SUVs from the ship-yard. It was too difficult to tell, but she thought she could see the outline of a figure in the driver's seat.

Was it Asad or maybe one of his men?

She scanned the area and found another SUV just like it parked deeper in another alley. She couldn't see into the vehicle due to its position in the dark shadows, but she had a feeling it was similarly occupied. By whom she didn't know.

Adriana kept her feet moving. If she stopped, it would look suspicious, and she had the distinct feeling that someone was watching. She glanced up at the buildings to her left and right, hoping to catch a spotter carelessly poking his head out a window. No such luck. All she found were dark windows or ones that were lit but covered with curtains.

She skirted the little plaza and made her way around to the other side where another couple was in the midst of an awkward late-night goodbye. Adriana figured they were on a date. By the looks of it, the first one. The young, curly-haired man had his hands shoved deep into his pockets and was swinging one leg back and forth as if his mannerisms might somehow make the evening last longer.

The girl, a cute blonde with long, slender legs squeezed into tight jeans was acting similarly with her hands folded behind her back as she glanced down at the ground and then back up.

Adriana walked by, tempted to tell the boy to just go ahead and kiss the girl, but she shoved aside the thought and kept moving. It was none of her business. Besides, she had a job to do, and it wasn't giving dating advice.

She slowed down as she neared the entrance to the Imperial and looked over the sparse collection of patrons sitting on the patio under a striped awning. People were laughing, making jokes, and telling stories.

There was no sign of Asad.

Adriana knew it wouldn't be that easy. If he wasn't in one of the cars or on the patio—as she'd already determined to be the case— then he would be inside. The guy's message hadn't been specific about where to meet at the tea house. She wondered if the vagueness was deliberate—a way to set up Youssef. For what she wasn't sure. It was too crowded for an abduction, even though the place was clearly winding down for the night. If Asad wanted to take out his ally, there would be too many witnesses, unless his plan was simply to eliminate everyone.

The last thought sent a chill through Adriana's spine. Extremists didn't have an issue with killing innocent civilians. That meant everyone at the Imperial could be a target.

She turned left and pushed her way through the heavy forest-green door. Inside, the place held a scattered collection of people much like she'd seen on the patio. It was far from full, but nowhere near empty. Pungent floral and citrus aromas filled her nostrils.

Adriana slowly made her way toward the counter to put in an order, not because she was thirsty for tea but because she had to look like an ordinary customer. If Asad or any of his men were there and noticed her loitering without purpose, they could be spooked and decide to leave.

As she meandered toward the counter, she panned the room, taking note of all the faces. There, in the far corner nearest a giant window, was Asad.

He was staring out the giant glass pane as if watching the streets beyond, observing every detail and person. That meant he'd probably seen her. The fact she was still standing unmolested in the line to order was a good sign. He hadn't recognized her, at least that's what she hoped.

Asad appeared to pay her no mind, which was fine with Adriana.

She stepped to the counter and ordered a cup of Earl Grey. Then she moved to the side and waited patiently, doing her best not to look back directly at Asad. She couldn't help but feel like he was staring at her. Adriana locked in her gaze on the chalkboard behind the counter. It featured the full menu of various teas the Imperial offered as well as traditional English snacks. The cucumber sandwiches caused her stomach to grumble. She'd forgotten to eat anything since lunch, and now wasn't the best time.

A young girl with a swallow tattoo on her neck and a ring through her nose passed the steaming hot cup over the counter. Adriana graciously took the bottom of the saucer with one hand while holding the cup with the other and made her way over to a table along the wall where she could keep an eye on Asad from an angle.

She also made sure not to sit next to a window. If there was one thing she'd learned long ago, it was to avoid windows. No reason to give an enemy an easy target. She eased into the chair and slid her tea close to the wall. She leaned against the wall with her left shoulder as she took a sip of the hot liquid.

Asad turned his head and glanced at her, but he wasn't just looking at Adriana. He was checking out the entire room, eyeing every face exactly as she'd done upon entering. He seemed to pay no attention to her and went back to staring out the large window.

Adriana exhaled. She didn't realize she'd caught her breath in the moment Asad was looking her way.

She sipped the tea and waited to see what he would do. From her brief reconnaissance of the streets and plaza outside, there were only a couple of points she considered to be threats. The two SUVs certainly were. There was no way to know how many men were inside each. Then there were the windows, but that was something she couldn't do anything about. If there was a sniper waiting up in one of the buildings and she made a play for Asad, the shooter would cut her down with ease.

No sense in worrying about things she couldn't change.

She checked her watch and noted it was a quarter 'til. Fifteen minutes until Youssef was supposed to meet Asad; only he didn't know Youssef wouldn't be coming. As if right on cue, Asad stole a short glance at his phone. Adriana could tell the man was getting more frustrated by the minute. She kept her gaze toward the entrance since it afforded her the ability to both watch her target and make sure no one burst through to cause trouble.

Five minutes passed. Ten. Twelve. Finally, after what seemed more like an hour, the clock on the tower in the plaza struck 1:00. Asad promptly pulled out his phone and tapped away at the screen. Then he stood up and stalked out of the room with an infuriated scowl on his face.

Youssef's phone vibrated in her pocket. She waited until he'd passed through the exit before looking at the message.

"You have crossed me," it said. "And you have worn out your London welcome. My men and I will hunt you down like a dog. You have betrayed not only me but the Red Ring."

Adriana's pulse quickened. If she followed Asad out into the plaza, she'd be an easy target—and he'd see her coming. If she could lure him, though, somewhere secretive, perhaps she'd have a chance. She needed to get Asad alone in a confined space where his goons couldn't come to his aid.

She stopped thinking and hurried down a narrow hallway in the back of the building. It led to the restrooms, the door to the kitchen, and a rear exit. She barged through the exit and out into the cool night. There was a tall wooden fence around the area she assumed was for employees to park their cars. A big metal dumpster was off to the right.

Adriana typed a short message into the phone: *I'm in the back, past the bathrooms, in the car park for employees.*

She stepped around behind the dumpster, doing her best to ignore the pungent odors wafting out of it, and crouched in the shadows.

Every tiny sound startled her: brakes on a truck, people laughing, a car door slamming shut. Adriana stayed patient. She held her weapon near her face and watched the rear door of the tea house until it finally burst open.

Asad stood in the light, looking more intimidating than he had before. Adriana told herself it was due to context. In the tea shop, he was just another customer. Back here, in the dark and alone, he was the enemy and a deadly one at that.

"Youssef?" he said as he looked around the space. He took another step out and let the door close behind him.

Adriana could make out the pistol in his hand, dangling by his side.

"Are you back here? It's me, Camir. I didn't mean to scare you with my text. I apologize. I didn't realize you wanted to meet somewhere so...private." He caught a whiff of the garbage bin and put a scarf over his nose. "We were attacked at the shipyard. If you weren't the one responsible, then we can work this out. Youssef?"

He took another step out into the open and wandered slowly toward one of the three cars to his left. The second his back was turned, Adriana stood up from her hiding place.

"If you move another inch, I will put a bullet through your spine," she said. "The second one will be through the back of your head."

Asad froze in place. He started to twist his head around.

"What do you not understand about what I just said? Don't. Move." She gave the order in Arabic to make sure there was no misunderstanding.

"Who are you?" he asked in an emotionless tone.

"Who I am doesn't matter."

"That's true. Because soon you'll be dead."

Adriana crept toward the man like he was a venomous snake coiled on a forest trail.

"Where is Youssef?" he asked. "I suppose you killed him?"

So, he wasn't the one who had Youssef murdered. That was troublesome. It meant another player was involved. Neither June nor the Director had said anything about that—probably—she assumed because they didn't know.

No time to think about that.

"Drop your weapon, Asad. Do it now."

He laughed at her command with a low chuckle but complied. The gun dangled for a second in his fingers before he let it fall to the ground.

"On your knees," she said.

He raised his hands slowly above his shoulders and started lowering himself to the pavement. Once he was kneeling, she rushed forward and shoved him in the back.

He fell over prostrate, barely catching himself with his hands and elbows before his face smacked the pavement.

After a grunt, he shook his head. "I don't know what you think you're doing, but you've made a grave mistake."

She pulled out a pair of zip ties she'd stuffed in her back pocket and grabbed one of his wrists. "The only mistake I made was giving you the chance to surrender."

"Ah, but you did that because you want something from me. Isn't that right?"

She said nothing. Instead, she grabbed his other wrist and slapped it together with the first, then made quick work of the plastic strips.

Then she grabbed him by the elbow and rolled him over onto his back.

"Aren't you going to read me my rights or something?" he asked.

Adriana stared into his eyes. "I'm not a cop."

"I figured as much. Was worth a shot."

"Get up."

"You've made it difficult with my hands tied behind my back."

She smacked him across the face with the back of her hand. "Since I'm not a cop, I can pretty much do whatever I want with you right now. I doubt anyone will be coming back here since this place doesn't close for another two hours. So, I think it's time for you to start talking. Where are the missiles, Asad?"

"I have no idea what you're talking about."

She smacked him again. "I can do this all night if you want. I can do worse if you prefer."

He let out a sickly laugh once more. "By all means, hurt me as much as you want. I'll never tell you where the missiles are. However, it might be helpful to know that they are being prepared for a glorious attack."

"I'd say half as glorious as you'd planned."

He narrowed his eyes momentarily and gazed into hers to see if there was truth in them.

"So," Asad said, "it was you at the docks. You're the one who killed my men and destroyed half of our missiles."

"Where are the rest?" She brandished her pistol, pointing the muzzle of the suppressor directly at his nose.

His smile widened, showing off crooked, yellow teeth stained from years of smoking and drinking strong coffee. He pressed his head to the muzzle. "You're too late, little girl. Nothing can stop it now. Even if it is only half the warheads we wanted, it will be catastrophic. We will strike a deadly blow to the heart of infidels everywhere. And it is just the beginning."

She started to ask what he meant by that, but her question was cut short by a crippling thud to the back of her head.

Adriana slumped over on top of Asad and rolled onto the ground. The world spun in her blurred vision. Her head throbbed. A figure stood over her holding a gun. Asad scrambled off the ground and sneered down at her.

Another man appeared to his right.

"Want us to kill her?" the one holding the gun asked. His voice sounded like he was in a tunnel.

"No," Asad said. "I want to know who she works for." He knelt down on one knee, looming over her menacingly. "And I want her to see the world burn."

12

LONDON

Ice-cold water splashed over Adriana's face. She'd been unconscious since the blow to the back of her head. The sudden bucket of freezing liquid to the face changed all that.

Her senses heightened for a second, and the effects of the injury vanished. She snapped her head around, shaking the water from her face and hair. After blinking rapidly, she realized she was in a hotel bathroom, tied to a desk chair.

"Have a good nap?" Asad asked. He was standing in the doorway with his arms crossed. One of his goons stood by the sink, holding a bucket.

Adriana twitched her nose and frowned. Through the shivering, wet sensation, she smelled something foreign. Then she realized why she'd been out. It wasn't the injury to her head. She'd been drugged, probably while she was woozy.

She took a deep breath and exhaled through clenched teeth.

"You know," he went on, "I was wondering why Youssef was acting so strange." He held up the phone so she could see it. "Your messages were oddly short. Youssef was never so succinct, in any form of communication."

Asad turned to his henchman and laughed. "He could never shut up, could he?"

The other guy chuckled and shook his head.

"Shame you killed him." Asad's demeanor suddenly turned irritated.

Adriana shook her head. "I told you. I didn't kill him."

"Oh? Because I just got word from my men that he was shot several times and dropped down a stairwell."

"I personally don't care if you believe me or not. But if you have half a brain, you'll listen to me. Someone came after Youssef. Two men wearing masks. They specifically targeted him."

"You managed to survive."

"I was lucky."

Asad bellowed. "Really? You don't strike me as the type of woman who relies on luck very often."

"You'd be right to assume that." She squirmed in the chair. "I don't know why they were after your boy Youssef. What I do know is that I didn't kill him."

"But you did try to kill me. And you took out several of my men at the shipyard."

"A girl's gotta have some fun."

He grunted his disapproval. "Well, I promise you, we're going to have lots of fun tonight. First, you're going to tell me who you are and who you work for. Although I can tell from the look on your face that you have no intentions of doing so. That's fine; my associate here can be very convincing." He motioned to the guy standing next to him.

"We may start with some waterboarding and work our way up to removing appendages such as fingers, toes, legs, arms, and, eventually, eyes before we kill you. I do hope it doesn't come to such drastic measures. I'd prefer you simply tell us what we want to know so we can kill you quickly and efficiently—and with less of a mess."

She noted how eloquent he was. His wording along with the way he spoke gave away an educated background.

Adriana gazed into his eyes. "Torture me if you want, Asad. It's not going to save you."

"Save me? I don't need saving." He was genuinely confused.

"You need to listen, and you need to listen well, Camir." She paused to see how using his first name would change his demeanor. "Whoever these guys are, they're either after you or the missiles. Either way, I can guarantee you they're coming—if they're not already here."

Asad ignored her and shook his head. He pointed out the door to the window. "Bring her over here," he said.

She struggled against the bonds keeping her to the chair as Asad's henchman grabbed the back of it and dragged her across the hotel room. He spun the chair around, forcing her to look out the window. The curtains were pulled back to the edges of the rods, allowing a full view of the plaza below.

"You guys didn't take me very far, did you?" She recognized the cafe below where she'd laid the trap gone wrong for Asad.

"No. We knew someone was following us, but not who."

"It doesn't matter what you do to me. I'm not telling you a thing."

Asad pouted his lips and nodded. "Yes, we've already been through that. And while I certainly plan on having you tortured and eventually executed, I thought we'd begin with something a little less personal."

Her eyebrows lowered and pinched together. "Less personal?"

Asad turned to his guy and gave a nod. The man flipped on the television, and a moment later a soccer game appeared on the screen.

"Major match tonight between Arsenal and Real Madrid," he said. "European Cup semifinals. The stadium across town is packed to the rafters. Seems like a perfect place to test one of our new toys, don't you think?"

Adriana couldn't hide the horror in her eyes. He was going to launch one of the missiles at the soccer stadium.

"Sixty thousand people are there at this very moment, probably drunk and reveling in the pointless joy and agony of sport. You see?" He held up a finger. "This is exactly the kind of wasteful thing infidels like you support. Not for long, though. We will eliminate the nonbelievers from the face of the earth, and we will do it thousands at a time."

"You think there aren't people at that game who share similar beliefs with you? You're going to kill Muslims, too."

"Sacrifices must be made."

"So, you're willing to murder innocent people even if they share your crazy ideology?"

"No one is innocent."

She flashed a glance at her car key sitting on the desk to his left.

Asad frowned and looked at the key. "You want this?" he asked and picked it up. He examined it closely.

Adriana watched as her captor twisted the fob around in his fingers. He cocked his head to the side and inspected the little pad in the center.

"I see you're driving a fine automobile," he said and pressed his thumb to the biometric panel on accident. He tossed the key aside. "Well, you *did* drive it. Not anymore. After tonight, there won't be any more driving for you."

He turned to his henchman. "Program the coordinates and the launch sequence. It's time."

The crowd roared on the television as Arsenal narrowly missed a shot. A moment later, they started chanting louder than before, sensing their team was on the verge of a major victory.

Adriana concealed her thoughts with an angry look. Had he pressed the button enough to activate the response Henry promised? She'd know in mere minutes. For the time being, she had more pressing issues.

Asad's guy flipped open a laptop and started typing. The screen was filled with a map of the city. Circles wrapped around a section of London where she knew the soccer game was playing out. The circles must have been the anticipated blast radius of the missile. Thousands of people would die at the stadium. Many more would be injured.

Adriana waited until Asad turned his head to get a look at the screen. When he did, she twisted her right hand. The rope rubbed hard on her skin, but it was loose enough for what she planned to do next. Then she saw movement in the street below. Four men exited a black van and were walking down the street. Their faces were covered in black masks that matched their clothing. She could see the outlines of weapons hanging in their hands. No automatic weapons this time, but in the close quarters of a hotel those weren't necessary.

"This is your last chance," she said. "They're coming."

Asad turned his attention to Adriana and then followed her gaze out the window. He saw the men disappear underneath them and clenched his jaw.

"Start the countdown," he ordered the guy at the computer.

The man pressed a button, and the screen changed to a timer. It displayed just over twenty-nine minutes. Adriana glanced at the television and noted there were still thirty-five minutes left in the game.

Everyone would still be there.

Asad picked up a radio and pressed the button. "We have trouble. Front entrance. Take them out."

He'd no sooner finished his order than he heard the sound of suppressed gunfire in the hall outside. Asad's face filled with fear. "That's impossible. They just walked in." Panic flowed in his tone. "Get out there and help," he ordered his men.

Adriana sprang to action.

She planted her feet on the floor and stood. Asad turned, but Adriana was faster. She swung the chair's legs around, striking his face with one as she doubled over to get as much height from the blow as possible.

Asad's henchman reached for the weapon on his hip. She rolled onto the bed, pressed her feet into it, and did a full backflip toward the gunman. Before he could draw the pistol, the base of the seat struck him in the head and plowed him into the floor. The chair's bolts and glue gave way on impact and split apart like a cheap toy.

Asad rolled to his feet and reached for a pistol lying on the desk by the computer.

Adriana snapped her right foot and kicked his wrist out of the way. She shook a loose piece of wood away from her wrists and then freed her hands. Asad tried to grab the weapon again with the other hand, but she snatched his wrist, twisted it awkwardly, and pulled him away toward the window.

He yelped as she jerked him forward. He put out his free hand to stop his momentum, but it was too late. His head went through the glass. Huge chunks of the window broke free and fell to the sidewalk below, shattering into a million pieces.

Sirens screamed in the distance.

Blood trickled down Asad's face. Adriana held him by the back of the neck, forcing his head down so he had no choice but face certain death below.

"Where are the missiles, Asad?" she asked in a gritty voice.

"I'll never tell you, infidel. Besides, you're too late. The countdown has already started. Soon, the world will understand the power of the Red Ring."

More gunshots popped in the hallway beyond the door. Adriana knew Asad's men couldn't hold them off forever. He'd obviously stationed men at the door. How many, she wasn't sure. She figured there'd been more downstairs. They were likely already dead.

A heavy thud at the door followed by a low grinding sound signaled one of the men had been hit and probably struck the door as he fell.

"They're coming, Asad. Do you hear that? Your men are dying. Whoever these guys are, they will kill both of us. Tell me where the missiles are, and I'll spare your life."

"Spare my life?" he laughed. "I am prepared to die. Allah will reward me."

She shook her head and forced his down a little more. "Last chance, Asad. Where are the missiles? How did you get them? I want a name. Who is your connection?"

He only offered another laugh.

More muffled pops came from the hallway.

Threatening this guy with death wasn't the way to go. That much was obvious. He was fine with being a martyr.

He probably wasn't fine with pain, however.

She yanked him back inside the hotel and kicked him in the gut.

He doubled over and dropped to his knees. She kicked him in the side of the head and watched him topple to the carpet next to the bed. He was out cold.

Adriana hurried to the desk and grabbed the pistol. A quick check told her the magazine was full. She slid it back into the pistol grip and pulled back the slide to chamber a round. Then she slid to her left and looked at the computer screen. Only twenty-seven minutes left on the clock and counting.

She hit the escape button and found herself staring at a screen full of code.

Of all the foreign and dead languages Adriana could speak and read, programming code wasn't one of them. However, she'd seen enough HTML to know that buried inside the lines of nonsensical gibberish were things an ordinary person could understand.

She put her finger on the mouse pad and started scrolling down through line after line of code until she came to a sequence of numbers.

They weren't color codes.

She scrolled a little farther and found another set of numbers.

"Coordinates," she muttered.

She pulled out the desk drawer and found a pen next to a notepad. It took less than twenty seconds to scribble down the coordinates. A rapid check through most of the code revealed no other numbers of that kind, which further confirmed her suspicions.

She minimized the screen running the launch sequence and pulled up the internet. Once in the web browser, she ran a search for both coordinates. The first pulled up a map with the soccer stadium dead center. The target didn't help her. She already knew that much. She needed the location of the missile. If she could find that, maybe she could locate the rest.

Her fingers flew across the keyboard as another thud came from outside the door amid gunfire.

Another of Asad's guards had been taken down. The henchmen on the floor next to her started to roll over. She kicked him in the side of the head with her boot and sent him back to dreamland.

She checked the screen for the results of her second search. It was an industrial district on the outskirts of town. From the looks of it, getting there would take almost twenty minutes.

Not good enough, especially with what was going on outside.

Asad started to rouse on the other side of the bed. That gave Adriana an idea. She snatched her car key and shoved her phone into a pocket. If he wasn't going to volunteer to help, she'd make him useful one way or the other.

13

LONDON

Adriana grabbed Asad by the back of his shirt and dragged him over to the door. He wasn't a small man, and getting him to move took every ounce of strength she could muster.

He kicked and squirmed but was still too woozy to put up much of a fight. When she reached the entrance, she let go of his shirt, twisted the latch, and flung the door open.

Two men were lying on the ground. Another was on one knee, firing his weapon down the hallway. The second Adriana opened the door, he took his eyes off the target, looked at her with surprise, and then caught two bullets in the chest.

The guy fell on his back, coughed for several seconds, and then went still.

"What's going on?" Asad asked, still out of it.

"You're not going to answer my questions. So, I'm using you as best I can."

He started to struggle, but Adriana hooked her arm under his armpit. With every bit of leverage she could summon, she raised him up and swooped her other arm around his throat. She squeezed hard, forcing him to use his feet and legs to stay up and breathe. Then she jerked him backward out into the corridor and aimed her weapon in the same direction the dead gunmen had been shooting.

Two attackers were advancing down the hall, mistakenly believing they'd eliminated the only threat.

Adriana opened fire, emptying half the contents of her magazine in seconds.

The gunmen tried to halt and retreat, but it was too late. They were completely exposed, and all they could do was try in vain to defend themselves by returning fire.

Adriana cut them down before they could get more than one shot away. Now the question was, where were the others?

She got her answer almost immediately.

They'd been waiting around the corner, probably as part of their backup plan or maybe to cover the rear while the other two advanced. Either way, the men rushed from their hiding place and opened fire.

Adriana held the heavy Asad in front of her. His eyes went wide as the rounds flew by, at first striking the walls and door frame. Then one caught him in the gut. Another struck his right leg. She felt him get heavier and the tension on his throat increased.

It was all she could do to keep him in front of her body. She worked the pistol under his other armpit and fired blindly at the gunmen. The shots weren't even close to accurate, but they were good enough to make the shooters pull back for cover.

She'd been counting the rounds in her head and knew that there were only three left.

No way she could win that fight.

There was only one thing she could do. Run.

Adriana let go of Asad and fired one more shot at the end of the hall. Then she took off in the other direction. She heard more gunfire coming from behind the enemy's position. *About time the good guys sent reinforcements,* she thought. That didn't stop her. She had to find the missiles before it was too late.

Asad fell to his knees, grabbing his throat with one hand and his bleeding stomach with the other. He looked up in time to see the gunmen reappear. They fired their weapons repeatedly. The rounds tore through his body. He shuddered with every powerful blow until he fell backward over his lower legs in an incredibly awkward position.

His lifeless eyes didn't see Adriana turn the corner at the end of the hall and disappear into the stairwell.

The gunmen only caught a glimpse as she vanished. The next instant, they took off in pursuit. One ran straight ahead to follow her. The other rushed back into the opposite stairwell to cut her off on the ground floor.

Adriana flew down the stairs. She took them two and three at a time, nearly losing her balance on several occasions. Once, she almost slipped and fell on her back when her boot caught the edge of a step.

Her free hand on the railing was the only thing that kept her from a crippling injury, or at least one that would slow her down enough to allow her pursuers to catch up.

She reached the bottom of the stairs and burst through the door into the lobby. Two men were dead on the carpet near the main entrance. There was no sign of the concierge, though she had a bad feeling as to his fate.

Adriana turned to her right and took off toward the rear entrance just as the door to the stairs across the lobby banged open.

The gunman saw her just as she reached the door and raised his weapon to fire. He squeezed the trigger the second his partner emerged from the stairwell. The bullet plowed into the man's back and dropped him to the floor where he writhed in agony.

The shooter tried to correct his aim, but the door closed and she was gone.

Adriana pumped her legs. Adrenaline coursed through her as the flight instinct kicked into full gear. She hit the button on her car, and the lights flashed from the end of the aisle.

Police sirens were bearing down on the location. She heard a helicopter's deep, throaty rotors chopping through the air somewhere over London. Henry was right about the cavalry showing up. From the sounds of it, most of London's police force was on its way.

She jumped in the sedan, revved the engine to life, and wheeled it out onto the street. Blue lights flashed off the walls of the buildings behind her as squad cars arrived on the scene. They turned into the hotel car park and disappeared in her rearview mirror a second before she turned off the street and onto another. A quick look at the clock told her there wasn't much time left.

Adriana thought of the timer on the laptop. Last she'd checked it, only twenty-five minutes or so remained. She hadn't kept track of time while trying to make her escape, but it was easy to assume it took five minutes. The reality was it took less than that, but better to figure on less time than more. Thousands of lives were at stake.

She stepped on the gas, and the Jaguar roared louder. Up ahead, a red light had traffic halted. She spun the wheel to the right, guiding her vehicle into oncoming traffic.

Cars honked their horns. The other drivers desperately steered clear while she played a dangerous game of chicken. At the intersection, more cars were going through. She timed it perfectly, accelerating through the light and narrowly avoiding a black taxicab by inches, mostly due to the other driver seeing her and slamming on his brakes.

Adriana yanked the wheel back to the left and into the open lane. She was ten minutes away from the warehouses she'd seen on the map. Luckily, she knew a shortcut from her younger years spent in the city. The normal route would easily take twenty minutes, which would have catastrophic consequences.

She swerved around a cab and back into the lane, narrowly missing a delivery truck. Just before the next light, she cut the wheel to the right and shot across the lane in front of another vehicle and onto a side street. The sedan bumped its way down the alley. The driver's side mirror nearly clipped a dumpster, only missing it by a couple of inches.

At the end of the side street, Adriana spun the wheel and hammered down on the gas again.

The street was mostly empty in front of her now that she was off the main thoroughfare. This same road would be full at rush hour the next morning, but at this time of day she had it mostly to herself.

A quick glance at the clock on the dashboard didn't help her heightened anxiety, and her foot pressed the gas pedal into the floor as far as it would go. The buildings whirred by outside the windows.

This was going to be close.

14

LONDON

Adriana slammed on the brakes and slid the car sideways into a parking spot. The wheels kicked up dust and gravel from the lot just outside the old foundry. In front of the main building was the truck she'd seen at the docks in Felixstowe. This had to be it.

From the looks of it, the place had been a steel mill in its former life. A for sale sign hanging on the chain-link fence around the perimeter hinted at the future—it'd probably turned into some kind of trendy, upscale housing community when it was demolished and reborn.

She flung the door open and sprang out. She gave no thought to leaving the engine running. Right now, her issue wasn't the government's car getting stolen. It was saving Londoners from a massive tragedy.

Adriana sprinted across the lot to a metal door that was hanging open. She stopped short of it and looked around to make sure no one was watching, maybe a sniper positioned to guard the entrance from afar. There was no sign of trouble, at least not as far as she could tell.

She cracked the door open a few inches farther and peeked

inside. There were four men standing around a laptop. It was too far away for her to be able to see what was on the screen, but she figured it was some kind of connection to the launch sequence.

Where was the missile? She hurriedly scanned the entire warehouse space and saw nothing.

Of course she didn't see it. They couldn't launch it from inside a building.

That meant it was outside somewhere. She leaned forward, desperately trying to find any clue as to where the launch platform might be.

She found what she was looking for a second later. Huge cords ran from the laptop station to the outer wall fifty feet away from the men. That had to be it. If she could get to the launcher and disable it, she could deal with Asad's men afterward.

Adriana heard something crunch close by. A shiver shot through her skin. She spun around just in time to see a masked gunman approaching with a gun pointed at her.

The man motioned to her weapon with his. "Drop it," he said.

She sighed. How could she have been so careless?

She put one hand up and started to bend down to place her gun on the ground. She kept a keen eye on his face, watching him watching her.

"Check in, Patrol One." A man's voice came through the radio on his shoulder and distracted him for the one second Adriana needed.

He flinched at the sudden noise. The gun in his hand twitched to the side just enough to be misaligned with his target. Adriana fired her weapon three times. Despite being muffled by the suppressor on her gun, the gunfire sounded like a cannon in the dead silent night.

The gunman's chest sucked in the bullets, and he stumbled back in shock. One of the rounds must have hit his heart because he fell over on his side, squeezed his trigger once, and stopped moving.

The one shot he managed pinged off the warehouse wall and disappeared into the night.

Adriana knew the men inside would have heard the ruckus in the parking lot. She didn't need to look through the door again. They'd be hurrying to find out what happened.

She stuffed her weapon in her belt and grabbed the gunman's HK, then darted around the corner and out of sight.

Six seconds later, three more henchmen appeared in the doorway. They kicked it fully open and one of them stepped through, sweeping his gun around in both directions to make sure the area was clear.

Then he noticed his comrade lying on the ground with blood oozing out of his chest and the corner of his mouth. The other two men exited the building. One checked to the left and the other to the right. The guy who went left crept to the corner and hesitated.

He looked back at the other two who were busily examining the dead body at their feet.

His hesitation cost him.

Adriana had been lurking just around the other side of the building, waiting for her prey to step into her trap. She grabbed the barrel of his weapon and jerked him forward while twisting the muzzle away from her body.

His trigger finger twitched, but it was too late. The gun had been pulled away from him, and so all he gripped was air. His momentum carried him straight into her arms. He put up an elbow to block a potential punch, but none came. Instead, she drove her knee into his groin.

He lurched forward, doubling over at the hips in agony. Her movement was swift and lethal. She stepped around behind him, wrapped her hands around his head, and snapped it to the side. The neck popped, and the man instantly dropped to the ground.

She didn't wait for the others to come looking for him. Adriana poked her head around the corner and saw one of the men still examining the dead man and the other moving along the wall toward the far corner.

Adriana stepped out from cover and took aim. She eliminated the closer target first, placing one shot in the side of his head. He slumped over on top of the man he was checking. The other one heard the shot and spun around to defend himself. His reaction was too slow. Adriana squeezed the trigger once, twice, three times instead of pulling it once and letting it go full auto. She knew the weapon in her hands. It had the tendency to ride up with each successive shot. Firing one at a time kept it accurate and allowed her to put all three bullets into the gunman's chest.

He fired his weapon harmlessly in the air as he collapsed on the gravel. After he writhed for several seconds, his body stopped moving.

She turned her attention to the door and stayed on her toes as she approached. A foot from the door frame, she slowed down and pressed her shoulder into the wall. She held the gun shoulder high and waited for a second before she spun around and shoved the barrel through the opening.

The man who stayed behind to watch the launch equipment was gone. Adriana started to cross the threshold. A hand reached out and snatched the weapon then jerked her forward. Her grip was too strong on the gun, and she felt herself pulled inside. He raised his weapon to end the struggle immediately, but Adriana rolled on the ground as he fired.

The shot missed, sailing just over her back as she tumbled to the ground. He adjusted for her sudden movement but couldn't get the weapon aimed fast enough. She kicked a leg up in mid-roll and drove her heel into his chin. His head rocked back and he staggered for a moment, stunned. She scrambled to her feet a second before he recovered and tried to throw a right hook at his nose.

He grabbed her wrist with one hand and raised his weapon with the other, once more attempting to end the fight with one shot. He tensed his finger just as Adriana smacked his wrist with her free elbow. The pistol fired off to her right. It struck the brick wall and ricocheted around the room before it vanished into the ether.

Adriana kicked her knee out, aiming for his groin, but the gunman saw it coming and dropped his fist down, striking her thigh with brutal force. The blow sent a dull pain through her leg. He twisted his other hand around to take another shot. Adriana used his momentum to her advantage and snatched the barrel, wrenched it to the side, and reversed the direction the gun was aimed. The shooter's trigger finger snapped at a gruesome angle. He howled at the sudden pain and jerked his hand back out of pure instinct.

She lined up the sights with his forehead and took a step back.

He reeled into the corner, grasping the crooked finger in his good hand. He said something in Arabic, but with his mouth covered by a black scarf it made the words difficult to understand.

"Shut it down," she ordered.

His eyes narrowed. She could tell he was smiling under the scarf.

There was no time to waste.

She aimed the weapon at the top of his foot and fired.

The boot exploded into a bloody, black mess of leather, shoelaces, and bone.

He screamed at the top of his lungs and doubled over, grasping at the wound.

Then Adriana kicked him in the face and brandished the gun again, demanding his attention.

She grabbed him by the back of the head and jerked down the scarf. All he could do was whimper.

"I know that you're ready to be a martyr for your cause, whatever that means. But here's the thing. I'm not going to kill you. In fact, I'm going to make sure I do whatever it takes to keep you alive. Because the rest of your life is going to be a living hell by the time I'm done with you if you don't do what I say. I'm going to do to your other foot exactly what I did to that one." She pointed at the mangled wound. "Then I'm going to blow off your knees, your elbows, and eventually I may work on your fingers. Do you have any idea how miserable life will be without all those things? You'll be in constant agony, perpetually maimed, and will wish you were dead. Oh, and I'll make certain you're in a place where you won't be able to take the easy way out. So, tell me how to shut down the missile."

He shook his head. The guy almost looked like he was about to cry. "It requires an access code. I don't have it. I'm just supposed to guard it."

She sighed. Why couldn't things be easy, just one time?

"Who has the code?"

"Asad. Camir Asad."

She grunted. "Asad is dead. Who else has the code?"

He shook his head. "No one. Only Asad could shut it down."

She was running out of time. "I guess I have no use for you then."

He started shaking his head in protest. "No, please. Wait." He put out one hand as if begging for mercy.

Adriana had none left. These men were about to murder tens of thousands of innocent people.

The muzzle flashed. The round bored through his forehead and out the back.

"Sorry. I don't have time to wait."

She turned and hurried over to the computer station. The countdown was on the screen just as it had been on Asad's laptop in the hotel. There were still five minutes left.

A quick assessment of the equipment did her no good. She had no idea what she was looking at, other than the fact that it was a computer with lots of cables and wires running out of it.

Then an idea popped into her head.

She fished her phone out of her pants and quickly found the name she needed. It only rang three times before the man on the other end answered.

"What do you want now?" Raymond asked.

"A-Tak, listen to me."

"Oh, so you like the name now?"

"Shut up. I'm standing next to a computer that's about to fire a rocket at the Arsenal game. It's got enough firepower to wipe out several city blocks. I need to know how to shut it down."

"What?"

"There's a computer hooked up to the launch mechanism. This missile is going to kill a lot of people if you don't help me shut it down. I need to know what to do."

"I...I don't know what to tell you. I'd need to be there to see it."

She didn't hesitate. Her finger pressed the camera app on the phone and she aimed the device at the computer station. The count-down reached the four-minute mark.

"Oh," he said through the speaker. "Whatever you do, don't hit the escape button."

"Why not?" she asked. That was precisely what she'd thought needed to be done.

"Because they may have built in a trigger that will launch the rocket when that button is pressed."

"Okay, so what do I do?"

"This is going to sound like you're talking to the cable guy, but did you try unplugging the launcher from the power source and the computer?"

She shook her head. "No. I didn't know if that would set it off."

"It might. From the looks of that screen, though, I wouldn't touch the computer."

"I thought you were an expert at this stuff. Don't you have some kind of workaround or something?"

"Without being there, I don't have any way of telling what will happen if I start messing with it."

Adriana sighed. Close to three minutes remaining.

"Okay, I'm going to check the launcher. If you're anywhere close to that soccer stadium, I'd get away as fast as possible."

She didn't wait for his response before tapping the red button on the screen to end the call. She absently shoved the device in her pocket and sprinted across the room, following the cables all the way to the wall where they ran up the side and out through a broken window.

She peered through the glass. Just beyond the walls, in what passed for a courtyard, was a light brown trailer on wheels. A missile was fitted atop it, angled to the night sky.

The clock had to be under three minutes now. What could she do? If she unplugged the launcher, that might cause the thing to go off anyway. Adriana wished she knew more about these kinds of weapons, but it just wasn't her forte.

Adriana followed the cables into the base of the launch platform.

She didn't know what any of them did. Some were to deliver power. Others were for communications with the computer guidance system. She figured the weapon had its own intelligence programming as well, but where that was located she had no idea.

There were a few switches and buttons, a couple of lights, and two knobs. None of it made any sense.

She glanced at her watch. There couldn't be much time left.

Adriana grunted in frustration. It was the first time in her life she wished she'd learned more about rocket science.

"Think, Adriana. Think."

She remembered building model rockets with her dad when she was a kid. Those small-scale missiles were vastly different than the high-tech weapon before her now. From what she understood, though, the propulsion system was probably the same. It would be a solid rocket fuel motor. That meant puncturing a hole in the thing might not disable it entirely and would still allow it to pose a threat to the city. While the guidance system inside would direct the weapon where to go, maybe she could disable it so the thing couldn't fly. She read a warning panel on the side that said, "Verify shipping restraints are active before moving."

Shipping restraints?

She dug her fingernails under the edge of the panel and tried to pry it open. No luck. She needed something to open the panel. Maybe if she activated the shipping restraints, the missile couldn't take off.

Adriana spun around in a circle, unable to find anything that might help. There weren't even any large rocks lying on the ground.

Then she realized what she had to do.

She sprinted back through the building and caught a short glimpse of the computer as she passed it.

The screen displayed 1:07 on the clock and counting.

This was going to be close.

She burst through the door and hurried over to the car, hopped in, and revved the engine. She spun the wheel around and backed the vehicle up twenty feet. Then she changed direction, shifted gears, and spun the tires on the loose gravel.

The clock in her head was running. She turned the car around the corner. The back end fishtailed around to the right. Adriana corrected the steering and straightened the vehicle again. The engine roared as she pressed the gas pedal hard toward the floor.

She swerved around a pile of steel beams and nearly lost control on the loose gravel. Once more, her driving skills were tested as she pulled the wheel one direction then the other to keep the car on course.

At the end of the building, she accelerated through the apex of the turn. The headlights lined up with the mobile missile launcher. Her foot stomped the pedal again. The engine groaned louder. Adriana reached for the door handle and pulled it. The wind noise grew inside the cabin.

She was going fast enough for a jump to be potentially dangerous, but it was that or stay inside and ram an armed missile. Both options came with harrowing consequences. She chose to be clear of the crash.

At the last moment, Adriana flung herself onto the gravel and away from the car.

The sedan rumbled away as she rolled to a painful stop.

She scrambled to her feet and staggered toward the building.

The car hit the launcher in a violent collision. The vehicle bounced hard to the right and kept rolling another fifty feet until it struck the wall of another brick building. The launcher flipped over onto its side.

Adriana couldn't put much weight on her right leg, but she managed to limp around the corner just as the rocket's motor ignited.

She watched as the nozzle lit up with a bright orange fire. It was so bright that she winced and pulled her head back around the wall. A second later, the missile released from its housing and launched.

It sprayed fire from its nozzle and sailed through the air, but the journey was short. The weapon smashed into the wall of the same building the sedan had struck a moment before. A huge section of the brick wall crumbled and caved in. The roof partially collapsed over a twenty-foot cross section, but the building remained mostly intact.

Adriana waited for the big explosion.

It never came.

She swallowed and let out a long breath as she leaned against the wall and slid to the ground.

15

LONDON

Mere minutes after the missile plunged into the empty warehouse across the way, the police started showing up on the scene. June arrived in a black sedan. Two men in suits accompanied her to where Adriana was receiving medical attention at the back of an ambulance.

June approached with a wry grin on her face.

"I see you didn't leave any survivors for us to interrogate," she said.

Adriana shrugged as the paramedic applied a stinging ointment to one of the several cuts on her leg. "They didn't seem like they wanted to talk."

"It's a shame," June said, looking out across the foundry property. "Now I don't know if we'll be able to find another link to the rest of their organization. However, you did stop a dangerous missile from killing a lot of people, so I'll call this one a success."

"Thanks," Adriana snorted. "How come the weapon didn't go off? I did my research on that missile. It's got a massive blast radius."

"Indeed," June said. "I'd guess that when you redirected it into that building over there, it didn't have time to arm itself. Some of those things don't arm until they're on their way to the target. Of course, given your tactics, you may have just knocked a wire loose. Our people will take a look at the remains when they get a chance. Our main concern now is finding the rest of the missiles. There are still dozens at large. There could be many lives at stake, just like today."

Adriana waved off the paramedic and stood up. She put most of her weight on her good leg, still favoring the other. "So, let's go find them."

June smiled and shook her head. "You need to rest. Besides, we don't have any leads right now. And there's no quick way we can track down the rest of the missiles anytime soon. I'm afraid we won't know where they are until someone launches one."

Adriana dug her hand into her pocket and fished out a phone. She held it out to June.

"What's this?" June asked. "Other than a phone." She added the second part quickly to cut off any wisecracks from her counterpart.

"After I knocked the rocket off course, I went back in and checked the dead guy."

"The one in the building with his brains on the wall?"

"That's the one. I found that in his pocket."

"Were you able to access the contents?"

Adriana scowled. "Access the contents? You sound so official. No, I wasn't able to hack into it. But I know someone who can—in case you don't have anyone up to the task."

June raised an eyebrow. "You're not talking about taking evidence and turning it over to someone without security clearance, are you?"

"Me? I didn't say that."

June's lips creased. "I'm messing with you. Hey, whatever it takes to stop these guys. That's one of the perks of being with this agency. We don't have all the rules and regulations others are required to follow." June held the device out to give it back to Adriana.

She took it and looked at it for a moment, contemplating what might be inside.

"I'll be careful with it, I promise."

"I know you will. For now, you need to get some rest. Maybe take some meds to help you recover."

Adriana's head twisted back and forth. "No time. Like you said, those missiles are still out there. I need to find them."

"You need to get some sleep."

"Don't worry about me. I will. You'll have your people check out the laptop inside?"

"They're analyzing it right now. Had to get the all-clear from the bomb squad. Last thing we want to do is send someone in there with a booby-trapped computer. If we find anything, you'll be one of the first to know."

"Think you will?"

"Hard to say without even having a glance at it, but if I was a betting woman I'd wager we're more likely to find something useful on that phone than the computer. The phone will have recent contacts, calls, messages, that sort of thing. If you can get it unlocked like you say you can, we'll be in business."

"My connection is good," Adriana said. "He'll figure it out."

June paused. "Do I want to know where you're taking that?"

Adriana started limping away. "Probably not."

"Can we trust him?"

"Probably not," she repeated with a shake of the head. "But he helped me find these guys. So, reason would suggest he will help me again."

Adriana stopped walking. She realized her car was a mangled wreck being scooped up by a tow truck.

She spun around and faced June. "I don't know where I was going. My car is trashed."

"I noticed. I'll give you a ride back to your place. We'll get you a new car tomorrow."

16

UZBEKISTAN

The mood in the room was as dark as the lighting. Only a few candles flickered atop makeshift sconces.

"What happened?" a shadowy figure asked from the head of the table. He was dressed in black, like the others. His scarf hung loose around his neck. There was no need to hide his face here. There was a bond of trust between him and the other men in the room, but he was their leader, the one who organized their operation. And he was the one who'd given them their holy purpose.

The chamber was set up like a conference room, except it wasn't made for business. The Red Ring rarely called a meeting of their leaders. It was too dangerous. With Western agencies constantly scouring the earth for anyone remotely connected to the organization, getting everyone under one roof had catastrophic potential.

In this case, it was necessary.

"Someone intervened," another man said from the left of the original speaker.

"I know that much. I want to know how they knew our plan. And I want to know who did it."

"We're just as much in the dark as you, sir," a younger man across the table said. He had a thin mustache over his lips that wrapped around into a goatee. "It had to be one of the agencies from the West."

"Americans?"

"There's no way to know yet. The only report we have is regarding a woman."

"A woman?" The old leader's eyes perked up.

"Yes. A woman with brown hair. That's all we know so far."

"We must find her," another man thundered from the corner of the table across from the leader.

"And make her suffer," someone else added.

The room erupted in a series of roaring agreement.

The leader sat silent, hands folded on the table's surface. The noise died down as everyone realized he was considering their next move. They waited for him to speak.

"And how do you propose we do that?" he asked. "We're looking for a brown-haired woman somewhere in Europe or maybe in America? We may as well try to find a pebble in the desert."

Most of the men grumbled for a moment, their righteous anger tempered by the sobering fact.

When the room fell silent again, the leader spoke once more. "It would appear we are dealing with a ghost. If she can find a way to foil our plans this time, she can do it again."

"That won't happen," a new voice said. "Proceed as planned. This woman is a rodent, nothing more than a nuisance."

Every set of eyes at the table turned to the other end where a man wrapped in layers of black cloth sat purposefully separated from the others. He stared at the table and didn't look up until he was certain he had everyone's attention.

A scar ran from the corner of his right eye down to the edge of his jaw.

"How can you be so certain?" the leader asked.

The new speaker raised his eyes and stared straight ahead at the older man. "How does one kill a rat?"

The rest of the men glanced at each other with uncertainty and waited for the answer.

"You set a trap. Once the rat is caught, you kill it."

THANK YOU

I do this at the back of all my books, but my appreciation is always sincere. I just wanted to take a moment to say thank you for choosing to spend your time reading my work. I put one of these little notes at the end of all my books because I know that you could have spent your money and time on something else, but you chose this book.

I am honored and hope you enjoyed it.

Please swing by one of your favorite online retailers and leave an honest review. Those reviews help authors because they let other readers know if the book is something they might enjoy. Plus, reviews help readers decide on what to read next. It's a win-win.

So thank you once more for reading me. I appreciate it and look forward to entertaining you again.

Oh, and if you'd like to find out where the Sean Wyatt series began, visit ernestdempsey.net/vip-swag-page to get some of my earlier books for free.

Ernest

OTHER BOOKS BY ERNEST DEMPSEY

The Secret of the Stones
   The Cleric's Vault
   The Last Chamber
   The Grecian Manifesto
   The Norse Directive
   Game of Shadows
   The Jerusalem Creed
   The Samurai Cipher
   The Cairo Vendetta
   The Uluru Code
   The Excalibur Key
   The Denali Deception
   The Sahara Legacy
   The Fourth Prophecy

War of Thieves Box Set
   (An Adriana Villa Adventure)

DEDICATION

For my friend Mandy, who is just as strong and determined as any character I write.

ACKNOWLEDGMENTS

None of my stories would be possible without the great input I get from incredible readers all over the globe. My advance reader group is such an incredibly unselfish and supportive team. I couldn't do any of this without them.

My editors, Anne Storer and Jason Whited, must also be thanked for their amazing work and guidance in crafting these stories. They make everything so much better for the reader.

Last but not least, I need to give a big thank you to Elena at Lı Graphics for the incredible cover art she always delivers, along with beautiful social media artwork.

Oh, and thanks to my stylist, Monica, for always being such a good sounding board while cutting my hair.

COPYRIGHT

Made in the USA
Middletown, DE
26 December 2023

46825586R00076